LEMON

PUBLISHED BY TWIITAGA

Twiitaga Pte Ltd,
106 Sunset Way #02-40, Singapore 120106

www.twiitaga.com

Printed and bound in Singapore

ISBN 978-981-07-6776-1

•

www.lemonaderevealed.com

AUTHOR

WILL CHLUHO read philosophy and theology at an affiliate of Pontifical Urban University, Rome. He was a creative director who had served on several multinational accounts in Southeast Asia, including BlackBerry, Mercedes-Benz, and Singapore Airlines. He's now married and advancing his philosophical studies with the University of London.

PROLOGUE

• • • • • • • • • • •

"IT'S ALL OVER."

It was midnight. It was all that Prince said. The moonless sky beclouded his face, the howling wind obscured his tone, and the crashing waves washed out his words—the multitude could not tell his emotion. Prince did not say how he felt. He sat down by the sea, slapped the sand off his palms, and began to work on his hurricane lantern while the multitude stood motionless, watching and waiting. Then from the darkness, the voice of a little girl called out to him, "Prince?" The man hoisted his lit lantern toward the girl— she was soaked, wedged between her father and her mother, shivering in the cold. Her eyes, twinkling with a twin of hurricane lights, beseeched the man in unspoken words: *Where do we go from here?*

They were exiles who had confronted a pair of tornadic winds in the raging ocean. Under the orchestration of Prince, they had bound their rafts together to prevent the encroaching vortices from sucking them up and tossing them into the sky. Children clasped to women, women clasped to men, and men clasped to their boats and makeshift rafts to form an unwavering islet of defense against the swirling columns. When the storm hit them, Prince relentlessly rallied, "Head-on, head-on!" They fought to prevent the spiraling waves from turning the defense sidewise and capsizing it. The mighty wave trains propelled the entire tribe of people—men, women, boys, girls, and infants, along with their boats, dinghies, rafts, and oars—to *safety*; oddly, because the whirlwinds could have taken their lives and ended the tribal line forever. They were swept to a deserted island in the Pacific where they sprawled in groups, spent from the battle against the treacherous elements. They had escaped their native land, which for years had been held in the tyrannical clutch of King Molan. Now they needed a new king. They needed someone who could lead them into the future. They needed someone like Prince, the man who had led them to freedom. They had called him "Prince" not because he was of royal birth but by virtue of his courageous campaign against King Molan. Buzzing with hope, the people nudged each other, they rose, and they gathered around their leader.

It's all over. Whether Prince had meant the triumphant end of their weeklong ordeal in the ocean or his leadership over them, they could not tell. They waited as he lit the hurricane lantern.

Where do we go from here? Prince tried not to think about the girl's imploring eyes. He repeated wearily, "It's all over." Then he rose to his feet and withdrew from the multitude. The hurricane lantern in his hand ebbed with every step and vanished in the distance.

A quiet anxiety spread among the people: "Where's he going?"

*

THE LONE HURRICANE LANTERN flickered in the wind, swaying back and forth at a constant pace forward along the darkened shoreline. Prince, the future king, needed to get away from the horde, but the exiles wouldn't leave his mind. He was frightened at the prospect of leading these people into their future. Something told him that they would make him their king, and he considered every possible way to dodge what many would otherwise welcome, what some would even pursue with every ambition. The king's throne was for many the seat of the highest honor humanly possible. He regarded it a burden. For years, Prince had rallied secretly among the people to run away from Molan's enslavement. He had risked his life for no other reason than freedom; and now, in an ironic twist, he faced the prospect of losing it. He didn't have the slightest wish for a kingdom. He always thought that kings paid a hefty price to be where they are, that a good king must relinquish all his personal interests—including freedom—and carry the burden of his people's welfare. His legs were wobbly and his steps heavy, and his belly was growling for food; but he felt none of that, consumed as he was by his worrisome thoughts. *If only I were ambitious, this current plight would be such pleasure. If only I craved the power, this would be such a great prospect.* He considered fleeing into the night, going back to the sea, even if it meant battling another storm; but the eyes of the little girl, along with the many faces of the people—hungry, grateful, hopeful, and worried faces—beckoned after him: *Where do we go from here?*

In the darkness of the night, the future king needed to see the light. *How can I possibly build a future for these people on this remote island? Will there be enough food? Will the soil yield sufficient crops? What if the tyrant comes after us? Do we have what it takes to defend ourselves? What if the storm hits us again? Do we have builders among us to give us strong, solid shelters? What if people get sick? What about education? What wisdom do I possess to guide the people? What strength do I have to protect them?*

"Should I flee?" he murmured, his mindless gaze cast seaward.

The lone hurricane lantern strolled on without a resolution. Then it stopped all of a sudden. A flashing pin of light approached from the opposite direction. *Who could it be? Inhabitant? King Molan's watchdog?* Prince shuddered at the possibility.

"Friend or foe?" he muttered to himself.

In the darkness of the deserted island, the flashing pin of light met the hurricane lantern.

"We mean no trouble," Prince initiated. "Exiles," he explained. Seeing the strange apparatus that emitted the flashing light, he stepped back. He gripped the hilt of his sword. "What's in your hand? Who are you?"

The stranger replied clairvoyantly, "I'm not Molan's subject." He flipped the apparatus around so that the light pointed inward, and held it out to the future king. "It's not a weapon. It's an instrument."

Prince hesitated.

"See it for yourself," the stranger urged, stretching his arm invitingly.

Prince put his lantern down. He fixed a glare on the stranger as he reached for the apparatus.

"It's an electric light," the stranger edified. "One hundred years from now, that"—he nodded at the flickering lantern—"will give way to this." He pointed at the flashlight in the future king's hand.

"No fire?" Prince marveled.

"No fire," the stranger affirmed.

Prince instantly recalled one of the many fires caused by a neglected hurricane lantern that took the lives of a few families on his native isle. "This is safe," he remarked. He weighed the apparatus in his hand. "This is good."

The stranger, witnessing a friendlier disposition, extended his hand, into which the future king erroneously returned the light.

"No, you can have the light," the stranger corrected. He dropped his hand and explained, "I created it. It's not been perfected, though. Not yet. But it soon will be."

Prince was baffled. "Soon? But I thought you said a hundred years?"

The stranger smiled. "Time flies," he explained. "Have you not heard that 'one day is like a thousand years, and a thousand years like one day'?" Then he extended his hand once more.

The future king, now realizing that friendship was being offered, took the hand, unsure, however, if he should return the strange apparatus to the stranger's other hand.

"My name is Twiitaga. I'm an explorer," the stranger introduced himself while their hands interlocked.

"Are you a friend or an enemy of Molan?" Prince ventured.

"Neither," Twiitaga said plainly. "I don't take sides. Yet, I'm a friend to all, even though some people take me for an ominous intrusion."

"You're here alone?" Prince queried, his eyes peering beyond his new acquaintance, surveying the silhouetted profile of a three-sailed schooner.

"I came with eight others." Twiitaga craned his head backward at the schooner.

Prince instinctively aimed the flashlight at the monstrous sails but quickly realized they were beyond its range.

"You seem anxious, my friend," Twiitaga divined.

"How do you know my thoughts?" Prince exclaimed.

"Why else would you be away from your flock? Besides, your many queries are a sign of an anxious heart."

"And how do you know I have a flock?"

"You walk with heavy steps, as if burdened by responsibility. Is that why you're anxious?"

Enthused to put a face to such clairvoyant words, Prince pointed the light at Twiitaga, who held his hand up to shield the glare.

"I'm sorry," said the future king, immediately aware of his folly. He pointed the light away.

Twiitaga laughed and shook his head. "Not the first

time!" He laid down his huge duffel bag and rummaged through it. "You must be famished," he said. Then his hand emerged with a foiled bundle and he shoved it into the future king's hand.

It felt warm. Prince unwrapped the foil cautiously at first, and upon seeing the spring chicken steaming under the pin of light, he dropped to his knees and feasted heartily on the explorer's kindness, forgetting momentarily the hungers of his flock and the Herculean prospect of feeding them.

"You know what I think?" Twiitaga asked as he uncorked a bottle of wine and handed it to the future king. "You'll make a great leader."

"Thank you for the food," Prince said. He ate another whole chicken, slugged mouthfuls of wine between, and gave in to fatigue. He slept by the sea in the open all through the night.

*

"WHO IS TWIITAGA?"

The bright clear sky revealed the clueless expressions of the exiles.

Prince persisted, "Did you not see an explorer last night?"

No one had seen him.

"Surely you must have seen his schooner?" Prince spread

his arms to illustrate a huge vessel.

No one had seen it, either.

"The schooner!" Prince exclaimed and dashed along the footprints he had left the night before. He arrived at the site where he had met the explorer. He surveyed the long line of naturally stacked boulders extending from the coastal rocks into the sea, at the tip of which the schooner was previously docked—it was gone.

"The flashlight!" he remembered. He searched all his pockets but found nothing.

One of the men came running with a wooden box. "Prince! I found this over there," he reported, pointing at the boulders in the distance. "Is this what you're looking for?"

The future king took the box and opened it. It was the flashlight. He lifted the hand-sized apparatus and found a note in the box:

A LIGHTNING FLASH BLINKS IN THE NIGHT
AND ALL THE EARTH IS MOMENTARILY IN SIGHT
AND WE WALK ON INTO THE DARK OF THE NIGHT
UNTIL ANOTHER FLASH SETS OUR PATH ALIGHT

"A lightning flash blinks…" Prince murmured. He shut his eyes to ruminate over the phrase. *Is Twiitaga trying to tell me something?* Then he opened his eyes, which now beamed with the bright blue sky above. He exclaimed, much to the people's perplexity: "How can anyone know the future for certain? To think that I've been seeking omniscience all this time!" He shook his head and smiled. And he said to himself, "At every step, big or small, a flash of light is all I need." He examined the flashlight once more and, looking yonder where the schooner had stood, said quietly, "Thank you."

Prince gathered everyone in the open space and the people declared him their king. "When we escaped the terrors of King Molan," he addressed them, "I had no knowledge of this land. All I had was a glimmer of hope for freedom and life, and along with that, a little plan to survive the treacherous Pacific—bound boats and rafts. Needless to say, I had no knowledge of the whirlwinds that brought us to safety. If then the Universe has colluded to bring us to where we are, would it not also guide us into our future?"

It was survival that spurred the exiles to this island, but the whirlwinds that carried them here. After the new king made his inaugural speech, he decreed every old name the new inhabitants had to be abolished. They were reunited under one family name: *Ahio*, which meant "whirlwind." And he named his kingdom the Island of Ahio so that he, along with his tribe, would always remember the faithful providence of Life. For his part, he would never forget Twiitaga, the explorer. He remembered the food and wine from the duffel bag. He remembered he had fallen into a deep sleep. He could not recall the many things Twiitaga had said to him while he slept, but he remembered that deep sense of assurance in which he had rested—of protection, of providence, of peace. He would rule Ahio by these principles. The first king of Ahio would tell the story of the explorer over and over again; and he kept searching for Twiitaga the rest of his sovereign life. As did the kings who followed.

*

LEMONADE
REVEALED

. . . .

1

I HAD NO IDEA WHERE I WAS—everything was black. I gathered that I was lying in a puddle of wet sand, as it felt cold, coarse, and prickly all over my back. I opened my eyes, and the first thing I saw was a blinding light—it was piercing. I blinked hard to flush the tears out of my inflamed eyes, but they kept welling up. I could see three big men towering over me like curious giants gathered over their prey. The men flowed and ebbed with my teary vision.

Like me, the first of the three big men was white. He was glowing brilliantly in an aureole. He had white cropped hair, white brows, a white beard, and a long white frock. And there was something white fluttering by his sides, flapping in idling motion. *Are those your wings?* I wondered drowsily. The blurred white figure was afloat inches off the ground where the frock ended. *Where are your feet?* The light from behind his shadowed face shot piercing rays into my eyes so that I had to squint. *That must be your halo.* Intermittent lights in his eyes blinked with every slight movement of his head. His lips appeared to be nipping at the air. What with my water-clogged ears, I couldn't hear a thing. *Is that St. Gabriel saying, "Hail! O highly favored one"? Am I in heaven?* The sight of his little paunch, which raised the soft white fabric into a molehill, somehow had a calming effect on me. *Maybe I'm still alive.*

My eyes wandered weakly upon the man next to the blazing figure. He was stout and the shortest of the trio. His feet were firmly planted on the ground, as if he were a strong tree that sprouted from the earth. His copper-skinned, muscular arms shot through a shiny armor vest. His large hand was resting rigidly on the large hilt of a sword at his side; the other hand knuckled to his hip. He was all wet and heaving. *Did you just slay Goliath from the sea? Have you come to slay me?* A thin layer of black hair started from his chin and rose evenly up each side of his face to his head to form a handsome oval. A firm, short moustache glided across his face above his upper lip. I could make out the warrior's maturity in years despite his strong, regimented body, as his temples were grayed. *Or is that St. Michael's illumined insignia?*

The third old man was the tallest. Now that I was less teary, I could make out that he had green eyes and a caramel complexion—I thought the combination rather odd. The man's starched brown suit hung neatly over his broad shoulders. His starched brown hair, with streaks of gray, fanned above his forehead like a proud peacock's crown. I could tell from the combination of brown suit and white shirt that the colors were carefully picked to match his hair. Even his face seemed starched: he had a sharp chin pointing up and away from his neck, and a sharp, small nose pointed confidently at the ground. His posture gave off an air of self-importance, the solemnity of which was immediately toned down by a purple handkerchief flirting at me from his breast pocket. All in all, he looked starched from head to toe, save for his soft, tiny lips, which looked incredibly agile swinging his pipe in highly challenging maneuvers. He was holding something glittery and weighty, and it was chained to his suit. I inferred that it was a gold pocket watch. Something about this old man in his suit and his pocket watch suggested that I was still in this world. Exactly what made me think that, I wasn't sure.

I saw the man in the white frock utter something to the armored man, who nodded and lowered himself toward me. His rugged finger and a very big thumb came toward my eye. *Are you going to pluck it out and eat it?* I wanted to turn my face away, but I was paralyzed. Moments later, his finger and thumb disappeared and reappeared at the other eye. Then he withdrew from me into the distance and said to the man in the white frock, "The boy is fine." I wanted to heave a sigh of relief for two reasons—that I was hearing again and the giants hadn't harmed me after all. But my body was too weak and too shocked to move, to so much as sigh.

All of a sudden, I jolted out of my daze when for no

known reason I burst into hysterical laughter. *Was it a joke that I'd heard before my world went black?* The three old men were taken aback. Then they too burst into laughter, nudging one another with their elbows and knuckles. "All right, he's fine!" said one. The other said, "Maybe a tad…" His finger drew circles at the temple. "But he's all right. He's all right, I'm sure," said another.

Who are you? Where am I? What'd happened? I shut my eyes and dug deep into my memory. It was blank. And then out of nowhere my mind recalled a weak impression of a haversack. *My bag.* I gathered every iota of energy and spouted, "My bag!"

*

2

THE KING'S HANDS TREMBLED under his robe as his stately frame rose toward the podium. His sweaty hands clutched to each other to quell the tremors. His head was still, but his eyes were searching the crowd. He cleared his throat with discretion.

Boys sat cross-legged in the front, their eyes lifted toward the podium, reverently awaiting the voice of their lord and patriarch. The girls rested their chins either on dovetailed hands or palms that opened like a lotus, eager to hear their king in person. Men and women backed against the walls and spilled out of the door into the big open field. Every window was stacked with faces. They displayed an array of emotions—curiosity, anxiety, gaiety—but each with a telling sense of piety to their king. *Why has Ahio IV assembled all of us? Has something bad happened? Is there good news for us? Will I get to kiss his hand, or so much as touch his hem?* And there were men and women, mostly women, with cradling arms on the far edge of the open field, coaxing, pacifying, or punishing their infants into silence, for their king had something important to announce. It seemed even the seagulls had stopped shrieking, and the leaves hadn't rustled all morning.

The throng outside strained their ears to hear the tinny voice of King Ahio IV clattering through the speakers: "Protection. Providence. Peace. Never forget the three pillars that constitute the foundation of our kingdom. Never cease to work with our counselor to foster peace, our sugar trader to provide for the people, and our military to protect our land and sea. Continue to trust that whatever you need will be given to you, because"—Ahio IV cleared his throat once more—"I must go.

"Dear compatriots, I must go, with all of my royal family, to meet what fate we cannot now know."

The crowd collapsed into a cacophony of disbelieving murmurs. "What is this, a farewell?" "Where is our king going?" "Is he sailing off with all of the royalty?" "That's plain insanity!" "The sea is too dangerous!" "Where is the royalty going?" "Are they running away?" "Are we under attack by the tyrant?" "What will become of them?" "What will become of us?"

Ahio IV raised his majestic sleeves, and silence descended, first upon the boys in the front, then the girls, then the men and women by the walls, then the craning heads at the sides, and in an invisible wave, the hush flowed out of the door into the crowd beyond.

"Do not leave us!" a strong voice concluded the dying

murmurs.

"Do not fear!" the king responded. "The fate of the Ahio dynasty is uncertain once we set sail. We may return safe and sound. Or we may perish in one of two prospects: the unpredictable treachery of the Pacific Ocean, or the equally unpredictable temperament of Queen Molan—the tyrant—who, as we all know, has always set her eyes on our rich sugar soil. She has thrown down the gauntlet to me. And I shall rise to meet her face-to-face." The king surfaced his trembling hands from under his sleeves and said, "Look! I may be in fear, for this implicates the lives of my beloved family"—he turned up his voice—"but behold, fear shall have no dictate over my judgment, no control over my action. Fear has no dictate over me. And so it shall be"—he glanced over his people—"with you!"

The people raised their fists and roared in unison, "A-hee-o! A-hee-o! A-hee-o!" Their spirit of courage heightened with every cry.

Ahio IV lifted his robe and descended from the podium. Cries of "A-hee-o!" faded as the people dispersed into their daily affairs: one third off to the sugar mill and sugarcane plantation, a second third to their barracks and observation posts, and the rest to fishing, planting, marketing, nursing, schooling, child-sitting, and so forth. By and large they weren't too sure of the full extent of their king's predicament.

They started into the day like they would any other.

*

BREAKFAST WAS FOR THE KING a time kept by royal decree from the world's endless interruptions. Today, he had summoned the warrior and the trader. Ahio IV lifted the lid of a small earthen jar. He took a heaping spoonful of sugar and sprinkled it over his buttered toast. A bold, flamboyant voice filled the hall: "Life can be bland and bitter without *that.*" The sugar trader, in a western suit and a peacock crest, swaggered from the door to the king's table. "Your Highness," he nodded to the man at the table, and teased, "I'm sorry to intrude upon your *sweet*-tasting meal—"

"I have sent for you, Barnett," Ahio IV interjected, "to entrust my will to your confidence—I meant to say—competence." He withdrew a sealed envelope from his sleeve.

"Absolutely!" Barnett shot. "A trader like me is not the man one can trust. I perfectly understand." He then arched his scheming brows and breathed, "Why not then Ahiga, your favored warrior and most loyal servant, Your Highness?"

"I have no wish to laden a man of the sword with the yoke of the pen. The pen far outweighs the sword when it's put in the hand of a warrior."

"But"—Barnett watched the king from the corner of his

eye—"wouldn't the pen feel weightless, like a feather, in the hand of the French priest?"

"Unlike him, you carry our blood," the king said stoically. "Half at least." Ahio IV thrust the envelope at Barnett without looking at him. "Now go forth, and dispense the majesty's will as you deem proper."

Barnett bowed, hiding his flattered countenance as he did. He clasped the king's will with both hands. "Gladly," he sang.

"If I should find the seal broken when I return, I will not hesitate to raze your sugarcane and the mill to the ground—along with you. This will be read and carried out only if none of the royal family makes it back, do you hear?" the king warned solemnly.

"You and your family will be just fine, my lord. Queen Molan, the archenemy and tyrant—ha! She's just a fangless dog—a bitch—barking without the…bite."

"Oh, thank you," the king remarked. "And as always, yours are such words of comfort." He laughed thunderously. "Like your sugar, Barnett, your words never fail to sooth our wearied souls."

"My sugar is my life." Barnett bowed in exaggerated courtesy. "What with the wisdom of my fathers who've built two generations of the world's finest sugar mills on your kingdom, we can all partake in the finer things in life. Isn't it my—I meant to say—*our* sugar that makes our existence possible, considering the fact that the sugar trade finances the acquisitions of weapons and ships, boats and bridges, and almost everything else on our island? Sugar is our life." His index finger poked at the air to indicate a period.

"And for a different purpose, it's also that of Molan's. I certainly hope I will be fine, as you have said, but one must never put his guard down with someone as greedy as a lion, as sly as a fox, and as dark as the moon as Molan, 'Servant of the Storm,' is."

The king looked at Barnett for the first time since his entrance, and with a hint of affection bade, "Godspeed, Balm of Ahio."

"That's kind of you. Godspeed, Your Highness."

Barnett opened his coat with one hand, waved the sealed envelope at the king until he looked, and dropped it into the side pocket. Then he winked and swirled around.

A warrior in shiny bronze armor marched in quickstep into the refectory. He approached the king without so much as a glance at the passing trader, who shrugged his shoulders and sniggered indifferently.

*

THE WARRIOR'S SHORT, STURDY FRAME arrived at the king's

table. Ahio IV greeted his military deputy with usual esteem. "Hail Ahiga, my oldest but swiftest warrior!" Ahiga responded in a deferential bow, keeping his head down until the king granted dispensation.

"Ahiga," said the king.

Ahiga lifted his head.

"I thought I'd better let you in on my voyage," the king said as he walked to the tearoom where private audiences were conducted. He indicated to the two armchairs in the middle of the small room. Ahiga waited until his king was seated before he took the privilege. He sat with his spine emphatically straight.

"As I've warned every son and daughter, Queen Molan has always had her covetous eyes on us," the king went on. He lifted his brows and explained in a whisper, "Sugar." He sighed and continued, "Quite a handful, Ahiga. Quite a handful, this tyrant. She sent for all of the royalty to grace the marriage of her beloved princess, and I do not think that we should allow her any excuse to make an enemy of us. So it is that we set sail today and subject ourselves to the unpredictable temperaments of man and nature." Ahiga nodded without turning to face the king, his spine straight.

"The sea is an unpredictable place," the king continued. Ahiga nodded again, his body as still as before, as if a metal bracket was soldered to his spine. "And God knows what that tyrant has up her sinister sleeves."

At this, Ahiga turned to face his king, waiting for orders. But none came, save this: "Ahiga, my faithful servant, thank you for your unreserved loyalty to me and to my family. I thought I owed you my personal word of gratitude."

Ahiga's shoulders and spine dropped involuntarily, his eyes affixed anxiously at the king. He implored, "My lord, send me and the fleet on your voyage. You must." He ventured to propose, "I will lead the navy in an octagon-star formation to barricade the royal vessel. My lord, then disperse the royal family separately into the smaller fleet, leaving the royal vessel empty—"

"Good decoy!" the king interrupted. Then he shook his head and said, "But I'm afraid the approaching convoy of sails would signal a threat to Molan—another convenient excuse for her to sink us."

"What then, my lord?" Ahiga resigned.

The king laughed. "No, no, no, Ahiga. I'm more of the opinion that the tyrant won't dare harm us. I seeded a rumor across the sea that should she so much as lay a finger on us, I shall not hesitate to lay the sugarcane plantation and the sugar mill to waste." The king explained, "Do you not see, Ahiga—no sugar, no war?

"My greater concern is the elements. Owing to the Pacific's mighty winds, storms, and great white sharks, the royal bloodline is definitely at risk." The king shrugged helplessly and sighed. Then he looked at his deputy affectionately and drawled, "Godspeed, Ahiga."

Ahiga's old, sturdy frame rose in a flash, and he returned the king's blessing: "Godspeed, my lord." Then he made for the door, knowing that the king's mind could not be changed, and the sovereign will must not be altered; for the king, he believed, was infallible.

"Just one more thing, Ahiga," the king called after him. "The majesty's will is in Barnett's safekeeping."

The warrior nodded, and as he exited the king's refectory, he could hear only one thing that rang repeatedly in his head. The words at first nudged him, then clasped to him, and then etched into him, like an order that was mandated upon him by God himself: No sugar, no war.

*

THE FRENCH FATHER CUPPED his hand behind his ear. "Pardon me, but please speak a little louder, my dear lady," his gentle, husky voice pled. The girl of mixed blood widened her big green eyes, as if doing so would heighten her little voice. She nodded at every word that parted from her pinkish lips, "My. Last. Confession. Was. One. Year. Ago." She relaxed her facial muscles momentarily and simpered,

"Father."

The priest's face blossomed like a sunflower, his eyes shut into a blissful smile. "I said louder, not slower," he teased, and laughed heartily. "It's okay, I hear you. Go on, my dear lady."

"Can I ask you one question, Father René?" the girl pleaded.

"Whose confession is this—yours or mine?" René quipped.

The girl dropped her head to the side and pouted her lips. *This. Is. Bad.* "All right. It's mine," René relented. *Never ever say no to a girl.* He slouched into the chair, and his hands rested on his paunch, anticipating more than "one question." "Speak," he said in a brief and gentle note.

The girl glowed in delight. René shut his eyes in anticipation of her quiz.

"Which came first—the chicken or the egg?" said the girl.

"Chicken," René said, his eyes still shut.

Gotcha, she thought. "But the chicken came from the egg!"

The priest was tempted to laugh but held it back and said, "Egg, then."

Checkmate! "But the egg came from the chicken!" Her face turned into a glorious grin. "So?"

Okay, if you insist. "In order for anything to exist at all,"

René ventured, "there has to be intelligence. There has to be"—his finger pointed to his temple—"a mind. Because nothing comes to be without a plan, without an 'end' in mind. Tell me, can you make a sandcastle without first having the sandcastle in your mind?" He paused to let her muse over it, which allowed her to conjure up her next question and the question after the next. She said nothing. She just smiled.

The priest continued, "My dear Chloe, it's more likely the chicken came first because, unlike the egg, it has some level of intelligence no matter that it's a bird's brain—still, it's a brain. However, it's not impossible that the egg came first, if we allow that the mind in which the idea of the egg was first conceived lies outside of the egg—"

"Father, how deep, exactly, is the ocean?" the girl interjected.

René took a quick peek at his watch.

"Father, why do people have different eye colors?"

He peered through the window to see how many more "confessions" he had for the day.

"Father, why does my maid cry whenever she chops onions?"

He made a quick headcount—forty-something!

"Father, how many stars are there in the sky? Do ghosts exist? Are there angels? Why—"

"Okay, time's up! We'll chat again, Chloe. Go in God's peace."

The girl was gone in a flash.

René shook his head in amusement and shouted to the window, "Next, please!" Then looking at the line of young confessors again, the old man muttered, "I'll be dead by noon."

*

"THE KING'S DOWN!"

Upon hearing these words, the warrior panicked and summoned the navy immediately; the trader dispersed his business confreres abruptly; and the French Father, worn out by children who had clamored for his undivided attention, returned to his siesta.

The trader and the warrior arrived at the watchtower: Barnett to confirm if the king's seal must be broken to disclose the will, and Ahiga to interrogate the watchman on duty.

"Where's Father René?" Ahiga asked as the two men climbed the watchtower.

"Siesta. Where else?" Barnett replied brusquely. "When is he awake, ever? Not even if Eurus drops by for a duel."

The nervous watchman overheard the conversation and

thought he had found his life-saving story: Eurus, the easterly wind of terror. He reeled up his sleeping mat, tossed it in the chest, and hastily tidied his hair.

"Soldier!" Ahiga bellowed the minute he reached the platform.

"Yes, sir!" the watchman replied.

"What did you see?"

"Eurus, my lord!" The watchman tried to conceal his nerves by shouting his words. He went one notch higher, "I saw Eurus taking down the royal vessel!"

"Why are you so sure it was Eurus?"

"Because," the watchman hesitated, then instinctively pointed to the right, "the terrible wind attacked the vessel from the east!"

"No explosion? No artillery? No trace of ominous presence?" Ahiga interrogated.

"No, sir!" the watchman shouted even louder.

"You're lying!" Barnett barked. He lowered his voice to a sinisterly whisper. "I see through you." Then he turned to Ahiga's ear and said, "The king warned me about Molan."

"The truth, soldier!" Ahiga pursued.

"I...I...I..." the fumbling watchman stammered, "I saw...Eurus...no...a ship...Molan's coat of arms...the wind...I..."

Ahiga inched toward the watchman and shoved him

away from the chest. He took out the sleeping mat and flung it off the watchtower. "Guards!" he blared, "Take him away!"

*

THE WATCHMAN WAS TRANQUILIZED by the spell of nature. The hot summer breeze buzzed in his ears; the sun's sweltering heat blanketed his feet, his legs, his arms, his chest, and his face; and the smell of sea salt lazily lingered under his nose. He had dozed away in the Pacific bliss, oblivious to ominous clouds in the distance looming over the king's vessel. He was jolted from his slumber by several shattering claps coming from the ocean. By the time he sprang to his feet, the royal vessel had spiraled into the sea. A layer of foam over a patch of darkened sea was all that was left of the Ahio dynasty.

The black clouds above the ocean had spread to the Island of Ahio. Ahiga and Barnett perched on the watchtower, mindlessly surveying the ocean, in shock. Nothing. Not even the slightest remnant of the fractured hull or a torn sail. Two names shuttled back and forth in their heads: Molan, Eurus, Molan, Eurus... The summer breeze had turned into a wailing wind. The sun disappeared into dark, ominous clouds. And the sea smelled mournfully bitter. The ocean was black.

*

3

IT WAS BLACK WHEN I CAME TO the second time. I kept my eyes shut, as I was still afraid to see the celestial giants. I thought that if I feigned dead, no one would bother with my presence, and, if I didn't pose a threat, I wouldn't be harmed. While planning my next course of action, I listened to the environment. I could hear the hollowness of the breeze buzzing in my ears, the rushing waves nearby, and occasional shrieks from seagulls in the distance. I heard no voices. *Maybe the giants are feigning dead too?*

The heat from the sun was starting to scald my face. *My bag!* I remembered. After what felt like forever—not a voice heard, not a movement felt, and not the slightest clue of ominous activity—I ventured out of my fear through systematic levels of risks. First I wriggled my fingers and waited. *Safe.* Then I twirled my wrists. *Safe.* I was ready for the big leap—I spread my arms wide apart. *Safe!* My fingers explored the coarse surface surrounding me, hoping that I would bump into a bag. My arms moved downward. *Nothing.* Upward. *Nothing.* Sideward. *Nothing.* With courage from God knows where, I shifted my entire body, hoping to comb a new area. My arms moved downward, then upward, and then—

A giant paw took my hand. *I'm dead for real!*

Go away! I clamped my eyelids tight, thinking for some reason that in doing so the beast would vanish. Maybe some courtesy might help. *Go away, please!* And then another paw dropped on my shoulder. "Go away!" I shrilled as an incredible power from within sprang me to my feet. I dashed away without so much as a glimpse at the owner of the giant paws. I ran toward the sea. *No, sharks!* I ran toward the woods. *No, snakes!* I ran zigzag along the beach without a clue as to where I was heading but with every certainty that I must run *away*. And run, I did.

"Come back!" a racing voice rumbled.

Then it chugged, "Come back!"

And it choked and sputtered, "Come back!"

I must be far enough now. I stopped to gasp. I took three huge breaths, closed my eyes, swirled around, and opened my eyes. It was the brilliant man in white; he, too, was gasping for breath. He threw his arms up to funnel his sleeves down, shaped his hands into a cone, and shouted something through it. His voice was husky and soft, and I thought he said,

"Your bag!"

My bag! I wanted to run to him. *Wait—is this a trap?* As I wasn't sure of my next move, I bought time. I showed him

39

my ear and shouted, "What did you say?"

"Your…bag!" His panting words reached my ear once more. Hearing his voice again somehow made me feel surer. *He is human.*

Still undecided, I turned my head to survey what lay ahead. I saw a cave made of boulders stained with green, black, and brown algae all over. There were spooky-looking roots hanging over the entrance. I heard incessant squeaking and fluttering echoing from the black interior. I looked up. The sky was fading. Ahead of me: an army of vampires. Behind me: a half-bent figure still gasping for air, at the worst, an angel. I made for the latter. *Wise.*

I trudged toward the old man, strutting with as much courage as I could possibly pretend. My fears were lifted with every step as I inched toward him. His halo had disappeared, as had the blinking lights in his eyes. *Angels do not wear spectacles.* I was hardly three yards from him when I stopped. He removed his pair of round-rimmed spectacles and cleaned it with his soaked sleeves.

"My bag?" I queried.

He swallowed a gulp of air and exhaled, "Yes!" He twirled his inverted finger a few times. "Come, turn around."

I turned my back to him.

He shuffled to the shoreline and returned hurriedly with a handful of wet sand. I felt something sizzling on one spot on my back. *Right. He had said, "Your back," and not, "Your bag."* Then I felt his fingernail scraping my skin, and as he did, some slimy suction removed from the spot. I heard a thud. Something fell to the ground. It was a curled ball of flesh in deep red.

"Leech," the old man said. He pointed to a cluster of islets in the distance where leeches were found. "You must have drifted through them." He looked up to the sky. "It's getting dark. Come." The old man turned and walked, and I followed close behind. He was limping. I thought it must be all that chasing. I slid to his side and offered my arm for a walking stick, which his "paw" took without a thought. As strange as it was, his hand had felt different from before. It felt warm.

"Have you seen my bag?" I asked as I stuck my other hand out as if it were carrying one.

"No, no bag," he replied. "Just this." He pointed to a heap of clothes as we approached the spot from where I'd dashed off.

I pounded over to my clothes and rummaged through every pocket there was. *There must be something in here—my wallet perhaps? No. Or something in there—a vessel ticket? None.* All that I knew from the moment I regained consciousness, surveying the three alien-looking men, was that I didn't belong here. I knelt hopelessly before the pile of clothes and wondered aloud, "Where am I?"

"Somewhere safe, my child," the old man said. "Hurry on; it's getting cold out here."

I picked up my clothes and dashed after him. "Who are you, sir?"

"I'm Father René Guillory. 'Father' will do."

"Father?" I hopped two steps ahead for a better look at him. "You mean you're my father?"

He smiled and said nothing.

"Where are the other two...giants—I mean—big men?" I asked.

"Oh, Ahiga and Barnett?" He walked on in silence. "Fighting over boys, maybe?"

Fighting over boys?! Is that what they eat? Is it some wicked game they play? What do you mean, Father? Something told me not to pursue that line of questioning. I dodged the subject altogether. "Where are we heading, Father?"

"Dinner!" He delivered his menu between steps: "A nice, warm soup...Fresh vegetables...Steak."

I felt safer with each step beside the Father, and my belly began to rumble. *When was the last time I'd eaten?*

*

4

THE EASTERLY GALE GLIDED ACROSS THE SEA and swept onto the coast of Ahio Island. The wind swirled round the fishermen's houses, snaked through the woods, escalated up the hills, funneled into the valley, hammered through the wooden gates of San Tommaso, and flapped the thin white curtains of Father René's dormitory. Ahiga knocked on the door.

"Who's that?" René asked, half-awake from his sleep. He fumbled for his spectacles, slipped into his sandals, and lumbered to the door.

"Ha! Sleeping through the storm like the Good Lord! Our dear old Padre!" Barnett taunted.

René cheered, "What wind! That the Balm of Ahio should grace my humble abode, and you, too, the king's 'oldest but swiftest warrior'!"

The visitors were dead still and dead silent. They looked unusually grave. René came round to their somberness. "Come in, please. Tea, at least, gentlemen?"

Ahiga turned up his palms.

"Whiskey," said Barnett.

*

To: Ahiga Ahio, my oldest and swiftest warrior; Barnett—"Balm" of—Ahio; Father René Guillory, friend of Ahio.

Dear Fathers of the Island of Ahio,

I have charged Barnett to break the seal and bring to light my will should I not make it back with the royal family.

The decision to take my beloved family to sea is the hardest I've ever had to make as a king. I have turned this over many times alone and with the queen: we deliberated between striking Molan on the offensive and turning down her invitation altogether—among other strategies. But either way, we would be at risk of losing innocent lives. Accepting the tyrant's "invitation" is the only way to avoid incurring her wrath. We cannot ascertain if indeed Molan has any hidden motives for inviting the royal family across the sea, but I cannot risk the innocent lives of my people in exchange for my own, and those of my family.

Beloved Fathers of Ahio, I hereby set forth my will:

Brother Ahiga: I charge you—as an ancestral Father of the island—to take from me the command of the warriors, and to raise for us henceforth men of fortitude, competence, and integrity. You are herewith commissioned by royal decree as Military Commander of Ahio.

Father René Guillory: I pray you continue your remarkable friendship and indispensable guidance to my people as Educator, Counselor, and Pastor of our young flock.

Brother Barnett: Your sugar has been the "balm" of Ahio's souls. I cannot thank you enough for this. However, if Ahiga should gather enough evidence to prove that the demise of the Ahio dynasty is in any way caused by Queen Molan, I charge you—as an ancestral Father of the island—to burn down every stalk of sugarcane you have along with your sugar mill in exchange for the safety of the people; for only this can avert the avaricious eyes of Molan. Being the best administrator among the Fathers, you are herewith commissioned by royal decree as the people's Governor, and the people alone you shall serve.

I, Ahio IV, hereby thank you, the Fathers of Ahio, for your service—past, present, and future—to my people.

Your humble servant,
Ahio IV

*

BARNETT—THE PARADIGM OF SUAVE and the pinnacle of charm; the epitome of collectedness and cool; Barnett, the flamboyant one who had teased the royal crowns and gotten away with it; the "cleverest" and "most competent" of Ahio; Barnett, the "Sugar King of the Pacific"—collapsed helplessly into his armchair, the king's will in his hands. *Burn down every stalk of sugarcane.* It was the only sentence in the letter that mattered gravely. The disoriented soul rose and inched toward the window. He pushed his arm against the upper ledge and buried his forehead into the crook of his elbow. His eyes darted about anxiously at his possessions: the acres of plantation beneath, the flock of workers, the line of cottages, and his handsome fleet of automobiles—a roadster, three motor carriages, and two motor wagons—along the driveway.

"My sugar, my life," he murmured. He lifted his gold watch to his eyes. *Time is running out.* He dropped the letter unconsciously.

Burn down every stalk of sugarcane. Barnett fell to his knee. He untied and retied his shoelaces. *Burn down every stalk of sugarcane.* He stood up. He removed his jacket and put it back on. *Burn down every stalk of sugarcane.* He sat on the armchair, stood up, paced around, and sat back down. *Burn down every stalk of sugarcane.* He withdrew a pen from his pocket and uncapped it, then recapped it, then uncapped it. *Burn down every stalk of sugarcane.* He rose for his whiskey flask and attempted to pour the liquor without uncorking the flask. *Burn down every stalk of sugarcane.* He uncorked the flask and tipped its lip to the glass—nothing came out. *Burn down every stalk of sugarcane.* He let the flask slip from his hand and it crashed onto the stone floor. *Burn down every stalk of sugarcane.* He slumped back into the chair.

Solutions, not emotions. He remembered. He pushed himself up gradually from the armchair, as a stealthy lioness pushes itself up from its predatory prowl, and he inched toward the mirror. "Think, think, think!" he chastised his forlorn reflection. "Think, Barnett. Think," he urged.

He lit a candle and held the king's letter just over the flickering flame. *No, the king's loyal servant would have been told about the will.* He blew out the flame. *Think.* He walked meditatively to his bar. He clutched a handful of ice cubes and dropped them from a height into a lowball glass. He opened a new bottle of whiskey and poured exactly one peg. He swirled his glass. He sipped the golden liquor. And then he smiled.

*

5

THE GRILL HISSED FIERCELY as the flames rose to kiss my face. The priest had tossed a generous portion of red wine onto my hot plate of sizzling steak, its outside oozing and fizzling now with blood and wine. The smell of cooked butter and grilled beef rushed into my nose—I gulped a mouthful of saliva. My hands reached involuntarily for the fork and knife.

"One moment, young man," the priest said. Conveniently, I dropped my hands by the cutlery. I watched him glide in and out of the kitchen like an aproned waiter I'd seen somewhere. Now he came back with two wooden bowls of soup steaming at the surface. "One moment!" Then he returned with a tray of green vegetables, fresh tomatoes, and grilled potato chunks. "One moment!"

My stomach growled, secretly protesting against his endless one-moments.

He came back to the table with a bottle of wine and an empty glass, and sat across from me. *Finally.* I reached once more for my cutlery.

"Say your grace," the Father said.

"Your grace," I obeyed.

He chuckled. "No, I mean, say grace."

"Grace?" I said.

"Give thanks, you know?"

"Oh—thank you, Father!" My stomach growled again.

"You're most welcome," he said. Then he started some hand gestures, as if he was going to deliver a homily from the pulpit. "That's very nice of you to thank me...but...we need to thank"—he pointed a finger at the ceiling—"God." I looked at the ceiling lamp, which immediately burnt a blue spot in my vision. He went on, "You know, my child?" *He's standing up!* "Man feeds on cow. Cow feeds on grass. Grass feeds on earth. But no one feeds on...man. Man, therefore, stands at the top of the food chain, superior to all." The priest looked at me. "Yes?"

I was famished. Yet my hunger for food had seemingly been replaced for something infinitely bigger. My mind, it seemed, was hungry for Truth. "No," I objected, "lion feeds on man."

The priest burst into laughter. "Bright!" he exclaimed. Then he folded his arms and started pacing about. He stopped, gazed at me, and said, "Accidents do happen. Accidents transgress intent."

"Father," I sought, "are you speaking English?"

The priest chuckled. He thought for a while and said, "You see—a lion eating a man is an accident. It transgresses intent. It violates the law of nature."

"How so?" I argued. "I thought the lion is naturally mightier than a man?"

"Are there more lions hunting down men than men hunting down lions?" he quizzed.

I shook my head. "No," I said.

"Who then is mightier?"

"Man," I conceded.

The priest beamed from ear to ear. Then he mimicked, "How so?"

I shrugged.

He pointed at his temple and said, "Intelligence."

Inasmuch as I was utterly defeated, I felt momentarily thrilled. It was as though the little debate was food for something huge and hungry within me. Father René picked up his cutlery, which reminded me of dinner; and I felt hungry all over again. He pointed his fork at the steak and said, "Man feeds on cow. Cow feeds on grass. Grass feeds on earth. No one feeds on man. Yet, for all the intelligence that man possesses, he didn't plan the food chain, much less create the sun and rain on which everything—earth, grass, cow, lion, man—depends for sustenance.

"God did."

Father René swirled his fork over the food. "We need to thank Him for all this, lest we forget the truth about who we are, and where we stand in the Universe." He stared at his steak, which had stopped sizzling, and he said, "Bon appétit!"

"Thank you, God!" I said hastily, plunging my fork into the steak. I shoved the meat into my mouth and bit a good quarter off. It was soft and juicy. I closed my eyes and savored the strong beefy flavor bursting with a hint of burnt meat inside my mouth. "Hmm," I let out, not knowing exactly what it meant. The priest burst into laughter once again. "Salvation for the soul in distress," he murmured softly. Then he said aloud, "Give thanks, my child, give thanks."

I nodded profusely as I sank my teeth into the remaining meat. "Father," I ventured, while wrestling the food in my mouth, "you mentioned that the two big men were fighting for...*boys?*" I swallowed a heap of chewed meat.

"Boys!" the priest exclaimed. "Why, yes—boys." He swirled his wine glass and took a sip. "Boys, like you, are most precious on this island besides sugar—so they think. The commander—the one who saved you from drowning—is desperate for boys because he needs to raise warriors to protect the people. The sugar trader, too, has of late accelerated his recruitment drive. He needs boys for the laborious process of making sugar from cane. Ergo—the rivalry between the two men. Almost every boy on our island is either an 'Ahigan' or a 'Barnettan'," he lamented. He stared into his swirling wine and said to himself quietly, "Oh, well. I should learn to accept the things I cannot change."

I did not fully understand what he said, but I didn't want to be offensive. I just nodded and chomped away the rest of my incredibly delightful dinner.

The priest slugged his wine and quipped, "You will be precious in their eyes!"

Somehow that didn't feel like a compliment. And as if he perceived my unease, the priest hastened to add, "Not to worry, son. Never worry about anything, for everything shall be taken care of."

The old man got up suddenly and began whistling a happy tune. He walked to an apparatus with a big trumpet and a small metal arm. With a clumsy thud, he placed the arm onto a black disk, and the happy tune from the trumpet continued from where his whistling ended. I thought I'd heard the tune from somewhere. "What song is this?" I asked, chewing my last grilled potato, which tasted incredibly good.

"'Hilary's Song,'" said the priest. "Everyone in the Pacific knows the song. It's a song of hope. This, too, is salvation for the soul in distress."

Now that I'd fed on my cow, I felt a ton of curtains weighing down my eyelids. "Is sleeping, too, salvation for the soul in distress?" I ventured.

"A bright young man, indeed," Father René chortled. "I'll excuse you from dishes for the night. Come, put these on." He handed me a pair of pajamas. "Some kid left them behind after a camp. They're clean." He indicated a flight of steps with his head. "First room to your left on the second floor. Good night, son."

"Good night," I said. I climbed the wooden stairs, feeling dazed. I looked behind me and saw the priest shove a cigar to his lips and light it with a very long matchstick.

*

AS I EMERGED AT THE TOP of the squeaking stairs, I found myself in a dim-lit corridor, swaying lamps projecting menacing shadows on the walls. Shut rooms that felt slightly less eerie than prison cells lined both sides of the long and straight tunnel. I hesitated. *Father! Can I sleep with you?* Luckily, I was in the first of the many Godforsaken rooms. I dashed through the door and slammed it after me.

"You okay, there?" the Father's voice echoed in the hollowness.

"Yes!" I hollered. "No…" I whimpered to myself.

I sat on the bed and explored the room with my anxious eyes. My sight tiptoed across the floor and rested on the wall facing me. It climbed the burgundy space and arrived upon a wooden cross. I took a mental note to consult Father René about the little man on it with V-shaped arms. My vision climbed further and negotiated a sharp corner, almost bumping into the ceiling fan, which was spinning gently on its own. It plunged diagonally onto a writing desk, dashed across the floor toward a table lamp, glided down to a tiny drawer, and returned to where I started—the bed. That about summed up my heroic expedition for the night.

It had been a strange day for me. Flashes of strange events, faces, and voices came to mind. *Why did the Father say that I'll be precious in the men's eyes?* That did not feel right, somehow. *Where exactly am I? Who am I? Will my bag ever be found?* I felt lost, lonely, and tired. Then from beneath the planked floor, I heard the clanking of glasses, plates, and cutlery, which for some reason lulled me into a deep sleep, my hands clutching the pajamas.

*

I AWOKE TO THE SCENT OF roasted ham and fried egg. The Father was reading soundlessly from a very big leather book in one hand, his other hand resting on the little handle of a steaming cup. He lay down the book, put on his spectacles, and looked at me from head to toe—I still had the pajamas in my hand. "Slept like a log, it seems?" he said.

I nodded.

"Breakfast?"

I nodded and joined him at the table. "Thank you, God,"

I said instinctively. There were two fried eggs and a ham sandwich on my plate. I gulped the milk and got to my sandwich.

The Father removed his spectacles and returned to his big leather book. When I'd finished my breakfast, he lay down his book and guided my hand to my plate. "House rule number one," he decreed, "we wash our own dishes."

As I walked into the kitchen with the priest, I noticed another cross, a bigger one, above the kitchen's veiled entrance. "Who's that little man?" I asked as I raised my head and rolled my eyes upward, my small hands preoccupied with the stack of plates, cups, and cutlery.

He lifted the veil and waited until I crossed into the kitchen; then he said, "Food."

I almost dropped the dishes. "Food? That little man is food?"

"Did you not *feed* on Truth last night? *Feast* on Truth, you did!"

"Indeed!" said I.

As we did the dishes, he told me to "hang around" in the dormitory until he returned from classes in the afternoon. "If you leave the gate, try not to go too far, and avoid the woods—I don't want to come searching for you," he warned. Then leaving the kitchen, he started between steps, "Hmm…what's for lunch? Minestrone soup. Vongole pasta in white wine sauce. Pork cutlets. Vanilla and chocolate ice cream." He turned around and winked at me. Then he waved goodbye with one hand.

"Bye, Father," I said.

"God's peace be with you," his voice sailed away, then returned abruptly, "If you do happen upon a skinhead with an eye on his neck—best to avoid him."

"Wait, an eye on his neck?!"

The priest was gone.

*

MY DAYS WERE VERY MUCH the same at San Tommaso until one morning. I awoke to an empty table, without my usual ham, toast, and eggs; to an empty veranda; an empty bathroom; an empty kitchen; an empty dormitory without the Father. The priest who, for the past fourteen days, had been my guardian, my teacher, my tour guide, my chef, my butler, my chauffeur, my companion—my only companion—my father, and my mother, had left without a word. I panicked, pacing to and fro aimlessly, combing every corner of the house—including the fridge—for the man I thought I couldn't live without. *Wait, maybe he's gone to school early today.*

I dashed to the staff office immediately, my hair

uncombed, and my mouth yet freshened. The clerk, a gray-haired granny, held her finger under her nose and handed me a folded note, quacking like a duck, "It happens. He won't be long." I realized even the school was empty. I said thank you to the granny and sprinted back to my dormitory. The note was from the priest:

Hello.

I'll be away for a few days. Please help yourself to the fridge. There's enough to feed you for ten years! Recipes are in the kitchen cabinet if you want to be adventurous. Otherwise, just make do with ham and toast. They're the easiest.

Remember, if you must wander off, avoid the cave, avoid the woods, and avoid the skinhead if you see him. Keep to the shallow water, if you swim, to steer clear of the great whites!

As always, feel free to hassle the kind granny at the office if you need anything!

Father René

The priest came back three days later. He did not say where he had gone or why he had disappeared from me, from the school, from the world. I did not ask, either. Life at San Tommaso resumed with my regular ham, eggs, and toast in the mornings; my school lessons in the afternoons, which I listened to from outside of the class window (Father said to "stay low" until the "Fathers of Ahio" decided what to do with me); my occasional tours to the beaches in the evenings; and my steak and soup in the nights. On some sleepless nights, I would ponder my lost identity and wonder if I would ever find my bag.

*

6

EVERY CHILD IN SCHOOL LOVED RENÉ, for he cared for them like a father. "Father, can I be excused from school tomorrow? And the week after?" "Father, can you patch my uniform for me? My mum will spank me if she finds out it's torn." "Father, can you zip my shorts for me? My hands are oily." "Father, can you unzip my shorts for me? My shirt got stuck in the zipper." "Father, can I sleep today because I don't like math?" "Father, can you give me the assessment quizzes for tomorrow?" "Father, can you talk to Dad? He's having a fight with Mom." "Father, can you come to my house to chat with my dog? I think he's lonely." "Father, can I bring my puppy to class?" "Father, can I bring my pet snake to school?" "Father, can I bring my horse to class?"

René's answer was always the same: "Yes."

Everyone in church loved René, for he pastored everyone like a father. "Father, can you bandage my fractured arm and not tell my dad I fought with that bastard?" a teenage boy asked. "Father, can you pass this letter to that handsome boy next to the ugly one in the third pew?" a teenage girl asked. "Father, I loved your sermon on the Holy Family last week. Can you tell my wife not to scream at my children?" a man asked. "Father, can you talk to my husband? Because he doesn't care about our family anymore," a woman asked. "Father, can you look after my sick wife tomorrow, as I need to go fishing with my old friends?" an elderly man asked. "Father, can you come over today to repair my kitchen sink?" an elderly widow asked. "Father, can you talk to my cow? Because she hasn't been milking lately," a desperate farmer asked. "Father, can you sleep over tonight? Or the demons will come after me," a lunatic asked.

"Yes." "Yes." "Yes." René would answer.

"The hammock," René had said when a student once asked for evidence of God's existence. "The hammock gives us peace of mind, a sign of God's provident love. The hammock is the answer to life's many irreversible problems, a respite in the dense jungle of trials and tribulations." His hand had gestured in the direction of the woods yonder, where allergenic sawdust lay hidden under handsome silver oaks. San Tommaso, his school, no bigger than half a soccer field, had an obsessive inventory of more than twenty hammocks in every corner that had a tree trunk or a building column. The hammock was his answer to every burdensome "yes" he dispensed. He would not say no in order to avoid conflict and enjoy peace of mind. But he would never have peace of mind because he always said yes. The hammock was his way of shutting out the world. Sometimes he would go so far as to isolate himself on an uninhabited islet nearby, lugging with him a hammock and an endless supply of meat and wine. "I need peace," he would tell his staff, and disappeared for days, leaving the school and church suddenly "fatherless" without him.

*

THE HAMMOCK ON THE VERANDA swayed laboriously under the priest's weight as he lay between a wooden pillar and an obtruding branch of a banyan tree. *Was it Eurus, the typhoon? Was it Molan, the tyrant? Would she strike us now that the royalty's out of her way? Are we to raise a new king, a new dynasty? Who will be king? What will become of Ahio Island?* He closed his eyes tight to shut out the noises in his head, an arm arched over his forehead as if to reinforce his suppressive measures.

Ahiga sat motionless, staring mindlessly at Barnett's glass of untouched whiskey. "Where do you think he's gone?" he asked.

"He mumbled about a letter," René said. He turned his body clumsily to face Ahiga. "Should be back soon, as he said."

"I don't know. I get the sense that he's hiding something from us. Didn't you sense that he was nervous?"

"Maybe. But I am nervous, too." René flipped his weight back to resume the inert position, his arm returning to his forehead. "What will become of Ahio Island?" he wondered aloud at the ceiling.

No sugar, no war. Ahiga remembered the king's infallible edict. "I don't know. But burn the sugarcanes—we must."

"You think?" said René.

Ahiga made no reply. *Something's very fishy,* he thought. He tried to recall a reversed order of events preceding the king's fate: *The king urgently summoned Barnett's presence. Barnett's absence from the king's assembly. His secretive visit to the Isle of Molan. The king's threat to destroy his sugar mill. His ongoing irreverence for the king...Is he part of a conspiracy with Queen Molan? Is Barnett responsible? Did he murder our lord? He murdered the king!* Ahiga shuddered. "The king's letter!" he thundered.

His panic was met with René's tranquil reply, "What letter?"

"The king's will!" Ahiga rose from the table, his mind scrambling with endless possibilities as to what Barnett might do with the king's will. He thought aloud, "No sugar, no war! Has the king decreed in his letter to raze the sugar mill? What will Barnett do to the will? Keep mum about it? Alter it? Destroy it?"

"Fire!" the urgent voice of a messenger rang at the door.

René slapped his own forehead. "When will this ever end?" he blasted, and wriggled out of the hammock. "Murder, conspiracy, typhoon, fire. What's next?" He shuffled hastily between the study and the bedroom, emerging each time with a handful of belongings. "I'm quite done with all this! I came to Ahio for peace," he said as he dropped a small leather-bound book into a huge rattan case. "I avowed a life of peace." He deposited a pile of white robes. "I became a celibate priest to woo peace." He deposited a green clerical stole. "For goodness sake, I want my peace of mind!" He deposited a metal crucifix. "My hammock," he mumbled, and shuffled to the veranda. He returned empty-handed. "Too bloody big," he murmured.

"I left my homeland for the East, left the East for Dartsouth, and left Dartsouth for the bloody Pacific! For what, Ahiga? For peace!" He deposited a large book that bore the words *Confessions—Augustine of Hippo* and snapped the luggage shut. "I live for peace."

"And would you die"—Ahiga showed him an inch of space between his thumb and a finger—"a little for peace? Father, not now, please." Ahiga laid his hand on the priest who sat heavily next to his rattan case. "We need you. *I* need you."

"Die a little for peace? More like for war," René snapped.

Ahiga unlatched the door for the messenger. "Where is

the fire?" he asked. The messenger pointed south toward Barnett's sugar plantation, where a thick black smoke fluttered furiously in the evening sky.

Ahiga turned to René, "Father?"

René buried his face in one hand and bawled, "Leave me alone, please." He wagged his other hand at Ahiga and the messenger. "I need time to think!"

*

7

I LAUNCHED A SEARCH-AND-RESCUE operation for my bag, partly to escape the boredom at San Tommaso. I asked myself, "Where should I start?" Then I remembered the Father's caution on my second day here: *Avoid the woods.* I closed the gate behind me and found my feet adrift as if they were on a conveyor into the woods.

I was amazed at the sight of a silver oak tree for its sheer height. It wasn't very big—at most three feet wide—but shot an enormous hundred feet into the sky. I'd hear much later from the Father that the silver oak is useful. It provides timber for cabinetry, shade for coffee and tea crops, and a favorable place for bees to make honey. But I was warned too that its sawdust is highly allergenic. The Father, being the Father, had philosophized that human beings, like the silver oak, consist of both good and evil potencies. As I ventured into the forest, I noticed that every tree was just like the first. All of a sudden, I was surrounded by identical-looking trees—everywhere looked the same. I began to see the Father's wisdom in warning me against coming here. Yet I wanted to explore deeper. So I snapped twigs into L-shapes as markers for my trail. *If I don't get lost, I won't need to "avoid the woods."*

I was quickly getting bored seeing the same thing over and over again and wondered if San Tommaso was, after all, quite interesting by comparison. I was thinking of making my way back when I stumbled upon a sight that seemed to conjure up a memory: a tree house. It was perched on an old banyan tree—the only banyan tree amid the silver oaks. I found its lone existence somewhat enigmatic.

The Father said that the word "banyan" was derived from "banias," which means "Indian merchants," who were always seen conducting their business in the shade of the trees. Here it was too that village leaders gathered to discuss and dispute official matters. The banyan held significance not just for traders and politicians, but the religious as well. Some Hindus regard it as the sacred abode of deities, and the Buddha sat in its shade to seek enlightenment. What intrigued me most, however, was that the banyan is an epiphyte whose seeds germinate in the cracks and crevices of a mother tree. The Father once took me to a "forest" of banyans where there were hundreds of them spreading across a huge land. "How many trees do you see?" he quizzed. I started to count and re-counted each time I lost count. He laughed and said, "Child, there is only one tree." All the "other trees," which numbered in the hundreds, were in fact one and the same tree. "Human beings, too, are many but one," the Father philosophized.

I later discovered that the banyan is also known as a "strangler fig" because its roots clasp like a web onto other trees and houses, "strangling" its neighbors mercilessly. I wondered if that was an appropriate metaphor for the priest, what with everyone strangling the poor old man with their needs. The Father was likened to an angel who hardly said no to anyone. He shared with me his personal maxim, "never say no to a girl," though in practice, he never said no to anybody. Which was why children clamored after him, parishioners adored him, and his friends loved him. Which was also why he always needed to get away from everyone to sleep in his hammocks and why he so desperately needed his peace. I wondered if angels like him could ever fly even if they had wings, what with such an atlas of needs yoked to their tiny necks.

I saw a rope ladder spilling from the banyan tree house. The dangerous-looking, flimsily flitting rope had a peculiar spell on me, so that once again my curious feet got the better of me. I lifted myself up on the first step and bounced mightily on it. *Safe.* I began my climb, feeling exactly like a great mountaineer—one precarious step after another. The ropes were wide apart, so I had to stress my thighs at every step. *This tree house is not built for a child,* I inferred. The incessant chirpings of birds grew as I scaled higher. And there were the ruffles of leaves from the fortress of big trees all around me. And then out of nowhere I thought I heard a man's voice. I stopped and cowered. *Is that the "skinhead with an eye on his neck"?* I immediately regretted defying the Father's counsel to avoid the woods. "Why didn't I listen?" I flipped my back against the rope ladder, shut my eyes, and was about to leap off when a familiar voice thundered from above me, "Ha! Speak of the devil!" In the next lightning moment, I was atop the tree house. "Where is it? Where is it?" I screamed, and hid frantically behind...nothing. I shielded my eyes with my hands.

"Where is what?" the same voice queried.

Eager to find out whose familiar voice this might be, I peeked through a narrow slit between my fingers. It was the old man with the gold pocket watch chained to his western suit. I spread my fingers wide apart. He was standing between the armored man and the Father. I dropped my hands and said, "The devil?"

The priest and the man in the suit burst into gales of laughter while the armored man stayed emotionless. The man in the suit inched toward me and grabbed my head. "Come, let me have a gooood look at you." He lowered himself and peered into my eyes. "Bright! Bright!" he exclaimed. I stole a nervous glance at the Father, who specifically told me to "avoid the woods." He wagged his finger at me. I was about to apologize for not listening to him when he smiled at me. So I kept to myself. Then the warrior greeted me hastily—with a smile or a frown I was not certain—and stomped back into the tree house.

*

8

BARNETT HAD SET HIS PLANTATION ON FIRE. "Let me through," Ahiga commanded the large crowd that had flocked to the inferno. The onlookers parted like the Red Sea for the king's deputy commander and his convoy of armored men. The troop marched toward Barnett.

Barnett stood on a fallen tree in the distance, holding up a burning torch. "Let it burn!" he gestured to a group of men with pails, tubs, and water hoses, the sugar plantation behind him aflame, spouting fire and smoke like a beastly mammoth exacting vengeance. He saw Ahiga and his military in the corner of his eye, stole a glance to confirm he'd been watched, and quickly darted his eyes back to the crowd. He hurled the torch into the flames and blared, "Dear friends, let the accursed be burnt to ashes, for it has spawned a tragedy so great I cannot even begin to think about it, let alone speak of it. It is sugar that aroused the avaricious heart of Molan. It is sugar that sank the vessel of—" Barnett appeared choked with emotions. He could not complete his sentence. "It is our king's will," he thrust the letter skyward, "to burn every stalk of sugarcane. And so it shall be."

A shrieking voice pierced through the crackling inferno.

"The king's will? Has our king died?!" That sent the crowd into an outburst of disconcerted murmurs, drowning out the crackling. Ahiga signaled discreetly to his soldiers to barricade the crowd from the burning heap, sensing an impending hysteria. He trudged toward the trader who had acted on his own accord and soundlessly reprimanded him with a murderous squint of disapproval. He lifted himself onto the fallen tree and turned to face the crowd. He raised his arms for attention. The murmurs simmered. The burning crackles reemerged.

"His Majesty King Ahio IV and the royal family have gone down into the ocean," Ahiga addressed the crowd in an emotionless manner. "The king, the queen, and every prince and princess on the vessel—" All of a sudden, he felt like his emotions were pouring forth with his words, but he held back. He forced his voice up by several notches, "All royal members aboard the vessel have passed on."

The finality in his words plummeted the crowd into an abyss of shock. He tried to comfort them, but nothing came out of his fidgeting lips; he, too, was breaking down. It was as if the reality of his lord's demise had finally set in when he announced it with his own words. Those words spelled out to him the end of his undying allegiance, his sole dependence, his life. He plunged his sword into the tree on which he stood to prevent himself from collapsing. And then something strong and warm clasped his quivering arm.

"Brothers and sisters of Ahio, I mourn with you on the loss of our great king," René's husky but clear voice roused Ahiga from immobility. But the crowd remained in their abysmal shock. "Even as we mourn, remember the prophetic words of your wise patriarch before he parted," the priest pressed on. "He said that fear has no dictate over him—and so too it shall be with you. We will mourn, we will cry, we will accept the great pain of our great loss, but we will not fear!" The people began to lift their heads one after another. "The king said, 'fear has no dictate over me.' Fear has no dictate over us!"

Ahiga's fidgeting lips began to form his king's words, "Fear has no dictate over us," unsurely; "Fear has no dictate over us," factually; "Fear has no dictate over us!" exclamatorily. The words spilled invigoratingly onto his barricade of soldiers, the water-bearers, the crowd from the front to the back, and to the despairing crowd far behind who were dispersing, retreating, escaping from the shock of loss. They turned around to rouse the king's edifying, exhorting, exalting words: "Fear has no dictate over us" into a deafening crescendo. The beastly inferno, voraciously consuming every stalk of sugarcane, was now a towering campfire that rose to the sky with the people's cry.

Suddenly, a worker smothered in hungry fires galloped

wildly out of the burning plantation and collapsed onto the earth. The audience in the front rows held their breath. Those at the back, spared of this horrific sight, chanted on: "Fear has no dictate over us!" Barnett panicked and hastily slipped the king's letter into Ahiga's hand. He ran, berserk, toward a supervisor and jerked him fiercely at the lapel. "Did I not tell you to clear the field?! You fool!" He shoved the supervisor to the ground and disappeared into the crowd.

The firefighters desperately doused the living torch, who squirmed, writhed, and fell motionless. Ahiga dashed forward. He planted a finger to the man's nose. Nothing. He felt the charred neck. Nothing. He dropped his head and said, "He's gone."

*

9

I SAT IN THE TREE HOUSE on a big, solid stool that was cleverly made from an old oak trunk. The man in the western suit rose from his seat. "Young man," he said to me as he smiled, "we were just discussing your future when you kind of broke in." Somehow, that felt like a handsome dose of respect for me. He raised his rugged hand, which was all too rugged for his fine manner of speaking, and he said, "Let us formally introduce ourselves even though I'm sure you're well acquainted with him." His palm swayed toward Father René. "And this is Commander Ahiga." His palm swayed the other way toward the warrior, who nodded at me emotionlessly, his spine rigidly straight. "And I am Barnett Ahio, the governor of this island." The man in the western suit introduced himself as if he was reciting an ode.

I waved at the men and said, "Hello," not knowing there were protocols to observe when greeting such men of honor as the military commander and the governor.

The governor laughed and continued, "You're in the Pacific Ocean, on an island called Ahio. We found you on a raft, if I may even call this"—he slapped his own pants—"a 'raft.' You had converted your pants—your pajamas—into a makeshift flotation device. That's very clever. We gathered that you were probably a trained boy scout of sorts, you being a tad young for the military. You were unconscious. But you came to on your own accord, and that was a good sign. The downside is you appear to have lost your memory, and that's a sign that you've undergone a traumatic—I meant to say—shocking experience. A shipwreck, perhaps? The waves swept you for miles. The wind brought you here. Do you remember anything?"

I nodded and then I shook my head.

"What's your name?"

I said, "I am…" My name didn't come out. I tried again. "I am…" Nothing came to mind. "I am…" I tried a third time—nothing. *What's my name?!* My tears suddenly welled up, and I wanted so much to cry aloud.

The priest rushed toward me and held my face close to his. "It's all right, it's all right," his gentle voice hushed. I could smell a stale mix of wine and fish on his breath. I wanted to turn my face away, but he held it closer. "It's all right, my child." I held my breath and let him express his sympathy.

The governor came to the rescue. "It's all right," he said to the priest, "let him cry if he needs to." He politely gestured for the priest to return to his seat. Turning to me, he grinned and said, "Not to worry, young man! I'll take care of you, if

75

you let me, and I'll ensure you get better with each day. Now, I don't want you to feel afraid or get too anxious. Just put your mind to rest and enjoy the sun, sea, and sugar." He grinned once more and added, "My sugar." Then he continued, "You'll probably recover from shock and recall things—your father, your mother, your name, your voyage, perhaps—in no time. I'll then send you back to where you came from, all right?"

I nodded, my warm tears dripping on my bare, cold feet.

"One of us here will take care of you. You'll get to choose. Can you choose?"

I wiped my tears and surveyed the three old men for the second time in the same number of weeks—this time to choose who among these strangers would be my father. My eyes rested upon the priest—*You're warm, friendly, and endearing; but I'll be bored to death at San Tommaso with you.* Next, I studied the warrior with much curiosity. I thought his eyes met mine for the first time. His was the silent look of empathy that neither respected nor pitied me; it was the knowing look. I hurriedly dipped my head to avoid his gaze, staring instead at his sword. *I'd love to play with that! But you're quiet and somewhat scary.* Then I examined the governor with the gold pocket watch—*You're nice and colorful and gentlemanly, and when you speak you sound like you're singing. I like you!* I supposed that my emotion betrayed me, because the gentlemanly governor gazed at me affectionately and said, "Looks like you've got someone in mind already!"

For some reason, I had the sense that among the three men, the governor was the one I could trust the least. I shook my head. "Well," he sighed, "that's perfectly fine for now. You have all the time you want on this paradise." Turning to the priest and the warrior, he said, "Let him bed-hop, perhaps? We'll take turns to host this"—he turned back to me and winked—"bright child of ours.

"Don't fret too much over things, boy. Enjoy your stay. Take your time; take your tours. It's a beautiful place. I'm sure you'll like it. Just beware of vampires in the caves and great white sharks in the sea." He shuttled his head curiously between the other two men. "And what else? Ah! And there's the madman rumored to be looming all over the island, feeding on bats. Just keep a watch out for any skinheads. There's only one, as a matter of fact. And that's about it, bright boy! Do let us know if you've decided on any one of us, hey?"

I nodded and looked again at the three strangers before me and the strange place around me. A sudden surge of emotion filled me. I missed my father, even though I had absolutely no impression of him.

*

10

THE TREE HOUSE BELONGED to the skinhead; he had disappeared from it soon after the royal vessel sank into the Pacific. There were rumors everywhere about his mysterious disappearance, some associating it with the king's death. But they were rumors. So the Fathers of Ahio—Barnett, Ahiga, and René—paid minimal heed to them, even as each had his own story brewing in his head. Among many things said, a handful had reportedly seen him in the vicinity of the cave; one story in particular recounted his diabolical diet of bats. The Ahio trinity concurred on the least dramatic point of the story: the skinhead with an eye on his neck was alive and roaming about on the island. Whatever the case might be, he had certainly deserted his tree house.

It had been several weeks since the three men had last met at the burning fields, which had claimed the life of an innocent laborer. René had withdrawn into an overflowing routine of extra-curricular events for the children. Ahiga had subjected himself to an aimless sword fighting, unarmed combat, and physical fitness regime. Barnett had consumed the greater part of his whiskey bar. The rest of Ahio Island— the jobless sugar workers, the headless military, and every man and woman—was getting more anxious with each day: *Will there be a new king among us? Who will lead us forward?* The people were not even sure to whom they could bring their questions. As far as they were concerned, the island was now without a king, without a head. Barnett, incognito governor, took the liberty to call the two men together in private to address the crisis and discuss their future roles. As very few people ventured into the woods, he chose to convene at the abandoned tree house.

"Will he come?" Barnett's quiet voice broke the silence, his whiskey breath filling the tree house.

René shrugged. "Perhaps," he offered weakly. He was feeling the need for his hammock with each passing minute.

"Have you seen him lately?" Barnett asked.

"He dropped by San Tommaso a few times, each time more silent than before. We had tea on the veranda and just stayed quiet all the while. He looked deep in thought every time."

"Did he mention anything about the king's will? Did he say anything about me?"

"Barnett"—René heaved a deep sigh—"exactly what are you up to?"

"What do you mean?"

"You razed your own plantation—your livelihood—to ashes. What do you mean, what do I mean?"

"It is the king's will," Barnett sang as he would a dirge.

"Only if Molan is convicted!" Ahiga's voice stomped into the tree house.

"When and how did you fly in?" René exclaimed.

"A warrior moves in stealth." He hurled a venomous glance at Barnett. Then he unfolded the king's letter and read word for word: "If"—he cleared his throat and repeated the word with vigor—"*If* Ahiga should gather enough evidence to prove that the demise of the Ahio dynasty is in any way"—he amplified the next four words—"*caused by Queen Molan,* I charge you—as an ancestral Father of the island—to burn down every stalk of sugarcane." He fixed an emotionless stare at Barnett and straightened his arm sidewise to hand the letter to René, who immediately dipped his head to vet the king's writing. Ahiga pointed his accusatory finger at Barnett and barked, "Has Molan been convicted?"

Barnett sniffed his purple handkerchief and replied, "Gentlemen, I have called for a meeting to discuss the people's desperate need for a new leader. If this remains unaddressed, I'm afraid they will begin to ship out very soon." He sniffed his handkerchief again, and said to Ahiga, "I would nonetheless be glad to answer your question, old boy. Has Molan been convicted? Yes and no."

René folded the letter calmly and said, "Explain."

Barnett complied with equal equanimity, "No, Molan

hasn't been convicted because we have no evidence, and I assure you there will be none. *However*"—he erected his index finger and wagged at the men—"I did have an audience with her, shortly after she invited our king to grace her daughter's wedding." Barnett dabbed his face with his handkerchief, and continued, "She said to me point-blank that she wanted Ahio for its rich sugar supply and asked if I would serve her should she acquire our land." Barnett opened his arms imploringly. "What does that mean if not that she'd had plans to sink our king and his dynasty?"

"Not credible!" Ahiga retorted. "Did she actually say she would kill the king? And if she did, do you have proof?"

Barnett's voice raised a notch. "What is this, an interrogation? What am I, a criminal suspect?" He suppressed himself back to calmness. "A criminal for obeying the king's will? Just what do I gain by destroying my own lifeblood?"

That was exactly the question that had driven Ahiga into near madness. He kept silent, still trying to dig deep into his reservoir of scenarios. Then he said, "I do not know," in reply to Barnett's rhetorical question, "but I do know that you have never been credible, never been trusted, never been reliable in conduct."

René thought he glimpsed a momentary smile on Barnett's face before the accused exploded at Ahiga. "For heaven's sake, the king's will was entrusted to my safekeeping."

He turned sharply at his accuser, "Not yours." Then to the bystander, "And not yours, either.

"Me!" he shot emphatically. "The king entrusted his will to *my* safekeeping. Are you telling me you have doubts about your lord's judgment?" He hurled his killer shot at Ahiga, which zapped the accuser's every intent to convict him: "So be it if you regard me a criminal, but what exactly is your charge? Arson? On my own property and livelihood? Defiance of royal authority?" His voice raised a notch. "Conspiracy?" And yet another notch. "Murder?" He thrust his hand forward as if to claim something from Ahiga and hissed, "Evidence?"

Throughout Ahiga's interrogation, Barnett's tone had swayed from friend, to convict, to prosecutor, and now back to where he had started. In the sentiment of a dear friend, he beseeched his accuser, "Old boy, what have I done that you must discredit my friendship?"

Ahiga felt like he had fallen deep into an enemy's trap and there was no way out but down. He wanted to leap off the tree house immediately; but he remembered the burdened face of each of his warriors, his family, and his friends, which now beseeched him in unspoken words: *What will become of us?* He remembered the king's will for him—and the other two men—to watch over the people. He had always prized duty above all things. He would now put duty above his unresolved suspicion against Barnett, into whose hands the king had entrusted the island's governance. Ahiga steadied himself and gradually lifted his eyes. He looked outside the window where the fortress of trees bowed at the wind's behest. He gazed solemnly at René, then at Barnett; and he said compliantly—and courageously—"Where do we go from here?"

*

11

THE WARRIOR WITHDREW THE BLADE from its scabbard and leapt two quick steps in my direction. He pulled all his weight down and sprang into the air like a spring released. He flipped his entire weight forward, his body curling into a ball in mid-air. As he unrolled his body, he cast the sword outward, simultaneously switching his grip so that the tip of the huge blade pointed downward over the head of an imaginary opponent. Then I gasped as I watched him falling in the air, unleashing all his weight with his steel blade at unrestrained velocity, its sharpened sword tip lunging into the head of the imaginary target. The warrior landed on one knee and let his sword fall onto the ground with an enormous thud. "The Flying Mantis," his voice pealed, proclaiming proudly to me the name of his gripping demonstration. Then he rose to his feet, hauled the hilt of the sword to his hip, and charged at me. I saw the tip of his sword coming at my face. I wanted to dodge but he was too quick. The sword's shining tip ended just an inch off my nose. I gasped once more.

"How long have you been sneaking at the door?" the warrior sought.

"I—"

"The Flying Mantis," he interjected, as he withdrew from me, "is inspired by the preying strategy of the mantis. Like the mantis that springs at its prey weightlessly and comes down hard and fast at its target's head, the Flying Mantis simply hoists the sword to a height and lets the blade fall through the opponent's head with maximum impact."

I shuddered at the image he'd given me.

His foot flicked the scabbard from the ground into his hand, and he returned the blade to safety. Then he tossed the sword at me with one hand and blasted, "On guard!"

I fell to the ground with the sword.

The warrior tucked his lips in, his nostrils widened as if his laughter was slipping through them. Then he lifted me up by the sword I was holding and dropped me back to the ground. He repeated his prank a couple more times, so that my whole body went up and down again and again. He seemed to delight in it, but he never laughed. Instead he said, "The sword is the killer; you are its instrument. Not the other way around." I felt as light as a feather as he snatched the sword from me. "Obey," he commanded, "and trust. This is the first tenet of the warrior's way." He switched from warrior to friend. "So you love the sword?"

I nodded enthusiastically.

"You need to eat, then." He grabbed the back of my neck and walked me to a breakfast spread laid out on a raised *tatami*. We sat, and I said, "Thank you, God."

To which he responded, "Father René is good with children."

We got on with a substantial supply of bread and meat.

I startled back, almost spitting the meat in my mouth, when he suddenly withdrew his sword again. He placed the weapon on the *tatami* and pointed to the long hilt. "Japanese," he said. Then he shifted his finger to the broad double-edged blade. "Chinese"—and then to the tip—"Western." His heavy finger shuttled swiftly between the hilt and the tip. "Eclectic."

I shook my head.

"Mixed-blood," he explained.

I nodded.

He nodded, too, and started out on what would be my first formal lesson in sword fighting. "The Ahio sword is unique in that it is the best of all worlds. The long hilt is modeled after the *katana*, but shorter than the original, to give you the flexibility of employing both one- and two-handed techniques. The blade is a hybrid—a combination— of the *dao* and the *jian*. It is broad like the *dao* to provide power at strike and defense, but double-edged like the *jian* to lend volatility to technique. The tapering and sharp-pointed tip is inspired by the rapier. This gives you a deep and penetrating lunge, flunge, or plunge." He spied me instantly to see if I was keeping pace.

I nodded.

He walked to his bookshelf and returned with a sword-fighting manual. "Here. It's all in here. Read—you must." As he tossed the book at me, which I clumsily grasped, he said, "Every warrior will be issued the sword of Ahio, but it is only those who complete the stringent regime and have proven themselves to be deserving of the honor who'll get to keep it. Once the sword is accorded, the sword never leaves its master. You need to know your sword as you would your wife, your lover."

He paused to let me muse over it, and resumed, "Questions?"

I nodded and instinctively raised my hand, but realizing I was the only student, I dropped it hastily, feeling a tad foolish. "May I ask things that are not related to the sword?" I asked.

He shook his head.

I wanted to ask him if there were people from all over the world in Ahio, since our sword was such an "eclectic" apparatus. "No questions, then," I said, to which he nodded.

Moments later, my inquisitiveness got the better of me. The words spewed involuntarily from my mouth. "Do people from all over the Pacific come to Ahio?" I pointed at the eclectic sword to suggest that the question was somehow related.

He peered into my eyes knowingly and said, "All right, granted."

He gathered the plates and bowls and put them to the side, creating a space in the center of the *tatami*. His hand hovered over the space and he said, "This is the Pacific Ocean." He took a teacup, examined it, shook his head disapprovingly, and switched it for a morsel of bread. He placed the crumb one-third below the midline at the center. "This is where we are, the Island of Ahio." He took the sword manual from me and positioned it somewhere top-right. "Dartnorth." He folded a napkin several times over into a rectangle, unfolded a corner so that its triangular tip protruded from the top-right edge, and placed it way below the breadcrumb. "Dartsouth." He added, "Father René came from here," his finger traced an imaginary line up and stopped at the breadcrumb, "to here." He placed a spoon to the west of the Pacific. "The Rising Sun." He looked at me and touched the hilt of his sword, and prompted, "*Katana?*"

I nodded.

He nipped a bigger piece of bread off the loaf and anchored it somewhere below the Rising Sun. "It's called Beautiful Island." Then he ran his muscular hand along the blade of his sword. "The place that inspired our *dao* and *jian*."

I nodded.

He chewed a mouthful of pork and spat on a spot northwest of Ahio. "Isle of Molan—stronghold of the tyrant, our greatest threat." Then he folded an origami pyramid and placed it several inches northeast to the lump of chewed meat. "Mikio Island.

"Ahio, Molan, and Mikio form what is known as The Pacific Triangle.

"Now, in answer to your question. There are those who came from all over"—his hand swept the air above the props—"and there are people from Ahio who left, some returning with new inspirations, others not returning at all."

"Why didn't they return?" I blurted.

He stared at me as if to suggest I was asking too many questions, but he relented. "Some had found themselves greener pastures, and others," he sighed, "did not make it back through the treacherous ocean."

I thought the warrior's voice cracked a little. He shook his head rigorously, as if he was shaking himself out of a secret reverie. Then he picked up the morsel of bread from the Pacific and tossed it into his mouth. He said, "It's easy for anyone to swallow us." He flapped my biceps. "Which is why we need to be strong, in order for us to protect ourselves. Train—you must."

I smelled tough times ahead in my days with the warrior. Then I looked at the map he'd created for me, which somehow had a profoundly comforting effect. I picked up my knife, sawed a morsel off the large pork bone, and dropped it into the Pacific where the breadcrumb had been. "A fortified Ahio," I said. I looked up at the warrior, who nodded approvingly.

"A fortified Ahio is my singular mission. Due to our rich sugar soil, the Molan regime has been eyeing our land for a long time. My great king always told me, 'No sugar, no war.' You see, in his wisdom, the most fortified form of defense is the deterrence of offense. I would not hesitate to raze Barnett's new plantation, if I had to."

I nodded, and then I shook my head.

The warrior looked at me and said, "Someday you will understand." He looked ready to dismiss me when a sudden thought seemed to strike him. "Child, you are new here, and I'm not sure how much Father René has told you about our island. But I'm obliged to warn you about a couple of 'mysteries' that loom over us. There's a skinhead with an eye on his neck—has Father mentioned this? The governor did, if you remember—the madman? The bat-eater?"

I nodded and felt a flush on my neck.

"My patrollers reported that he had disappeared mysteriously after our king's vessel sank. But recently, there have been sightings of this man looming suspiciously around in the woods, and he's seen furtively coming in and out of the vampires' den. People are saying that he's eating bats and living among them in the dark. I have seen him once with my own eyes in the forest, and just when I thought our eyes had met, he vanished into the trees. I'm not sure about what others have said, but my own experience tells me it is best to avoid the woods and especially the vampires' den. The skinhead, it appears, has turned into something else altogether—some say a 'sea demon'—ever since the king drowned. And I wouldn't rule out the possibility that he had something to do with the sinking."

My teacher warned me with a solemn glare, "Stay away from the vampires' den—you must."

I nodded until my head almost fell off.

"Dismissed," my commander said.

I savored the work of art on the *tatami* once more—the Pacific Ocean, Ahio, Molan, Mikio, Dartnorth, Dartsouth—and as I did, a deep sense of being separated, of being abandoned, crept in. *Where had I come from?*

"On guard!" the commander thundered all of sudden. Then I heard his sword rattling. I shut my eyes in panic and my hands fumbled for his flying sword. I felt nothing in my hands and opened my eyes—the sword was still in the warrior's hand. He rattled his sword in the scabbard once more and I fidgeted like I was having a spasm.

Once again, the warrior tucked his lips in and widened

his nostrils. In addition, his shoulders tottered to and fro, and his eyes welled up. He looked like a volcano on the verge of erupting into laughter. *Why don't you just laugh it out?* I thought. With the priest, I could speak my mind with ease, such as refuting his proposition with "lion feeds on man." With this armored man, I said nothing.

*

12

COUNTLESS CICADAS CLATTERED IN THE TREES, creating a deafening hum in the quiet night sky of Ahio Island. The full moon splashed a glorious light upon the naval barracks, its glowing grey surface starkly contrasted against black. It would make a handsome feast for an enemy's night assault. Ahiga, its commander, was sound asleep.

He saw himself walking aimlessly in the dark. He came upon a bridge, and as he climbed the steps, an elderly voice rose from beneath: "Watch your step, for I'm old and weak, and my joints are coming apart." *Bridges don't talk. It must be a figment of my imagination.* He ascended the squeaking steps indifferently. Upon arriving midway over the river, the bridge caved in and he was funneled into the cold water. He swam into a quiet cove filled with floating coconuts. The full moon lowered itself to lend its light, and to his horror, the coconuts all around him were in fact heads of dead infants. They started singing mournfully, hauntingly, "Feed me, feed me. Milk, bread, and honey…" *The dead don't talk. It must be a figment of my imagination.* He followed the moonlight and swam into the open sea, where all of a sudden, the waters gathered into a vortex and transformed into a sea demon, towering over him and spitting piercing flames at him. He ducked into the water, but a giant tailfin flipped him out of the sea and hurled him into the sky. A fiery voice gushed from the demon's mouth, "Behold! And bow before me, for I am Molan, the Ruler of the Pacific!" *Molan does talk!*

His body jolted violently, breaking into a cold sweat on his bed. Then he thought he heard three gunshots ringing consecutively in the sky, frightening the millions of singing cicadas into silence. He tried to decipher which part of this was dream, and which reality, when an army of scrambling boots arrived outside his barracks. "Gunshots! Gunshots, Commander!"

Ahiga sprang to his feet and donned his full military armor at lightning speed. In the next moment, he was in a truck with the warriors as it rumbled south on the dusty road toward Barnett's residence.

He tried to compose himself on the bumpy ride, recalling the scenes in his nightmare and what they might mean to him. He rested his elbows on his knees and pressed his confused head into his hands to shut the gunshots, the bumpy jerks, and every distraction from his mind. He immersed gradually into a state of calm. And then back into his dreams. *The talking bridge…* He remembered one of his warriors telling him about an aged mother who almost fell through a dilapidated bridge. *Infrastructure!*

The famished infants... He recalled an ex-sugar grinder he met days ago at the village market; the jobless man lamented about his depleted savings and undernourished daughters. *Economy!*

The fiery sea demon, Molan... He remembered an intelligence report in which Molan had stepped up acquisitions of military boats and guns ever since the king passed on. *Defense!*

He rubbed his face repeatedly. *I'm getting there...* Then he saw the light. The dreams manifested his anxieties—infrastructure, economy, and defense. His dreams brought to light the deep sense of helplessness and prophetic doom that had been nagging him for days and nights, but that had been repressed. He sighed in relief even as there lay no tangible solution before him. For him, nothing was scarier than not knowing the problem. Now that he knew the problem, he would find the solution. He would come back to this later. For now, he had something else to deal with. The gunshots in the night demanded his full attention. *What now, Mr. Barnett.*

The truck arrived at Barnett's residence.

*

13

I SAW MY BAG in the flash of a moment, in that infinitesimal fraction of a second when space, time, and two individual and mutually isolated lines of human action coincided—colluded—and combusted into what would become my life-changing moment.

My commander had taught me many things—tactical day movement, night movement, sword fighting, life-saving, first aid, and jungle and ocean survivals among others—most of which I neither took a special interest in nor thought important. I obliged nonetheless with ostensible interest for fear of disciplinary actions, such as the infamous "solitary confinement," which was routine under the commander's regime. My "excellent performance" and "enthusiasm" were rewarded with a break from the barracks. I decided to use it to explore the island. I wanted to know more about Ahio, as by and by I'd grown accustomed to, and was quite taken with, this idyllic and somewhat mystifying island. I remembered the vampires' den I'd chanced upon when I was escaping the clasp of "the giant paw," and decided to head in that direction, with no other rationale than to be random. *Stay away from the vampire's den—you must.* My commander's order rang in my head; but my feet, it seemed, had a mind of their own.

I sauntered along the breezy ocean and plunged into a sea of thoughts. I recalled the uncanny chain of events leading up to my chance encounter with the three old men at the tree house. I wondered if everything happened for an intended purpose, intended by something or someone other than those of us involved; or if everything happened as randomly as I'd taken the expedition at hand. I took a mental note to consult someone who may be wise enough to answer, and for some reason the face of Father René flashed in my mind. I saw him chasing a frightened boy, and I burst into self-deprecating laughter. *Silly boy.* I returned to the night when I was alone in a strange room, and I heard him washing the dishes, the clanking of which brought me immense comfort.

My thoughts advanced and arrived at the tree house, to the handsome voice and gentle face of the governor. He had so much charm that I'd almost chosen him there and then to father me. I got the feeling that my life would be colorful and vivacious with this old man.

Then my mind crept into the commander's barracks to replay his breathtaking "Flying Mantis" stunt, which almost cost me a fractured jaw from awe. I revisited the training grounds—the gym, the open field, the open sea, and the jungle terrain—where trainees like me were regularly meted out with "corrective" measures such as "one hundred push-ups!" and "water treatment!" Much as I didn't like the commander's regime very much, I did feel a certain sense of self-confidence, strength, and security through it all.

Who among you would be my father? "No hurry," I excused myself.

I had walked a quaint distance when a skein of geese glided at a height above me. My finger traced the birds in formation to write an imaginary V across the sky. I marveled at how a bird can borrow the lifting pressure of the bird in front of it, so it doesn't need to work as hard to stay in the air. I sympathized with the one in the front, who had no one ahead to lend it a lift. I wondered if they took turns to lead. I followed their line of flight and gazed into the distant horizon. *They wouldn't make it if they flew alone.*

A hermit crab tiptoed across my path in a curiously nervous gait and hastily disappeared into the sand. I knelt and dug at the sand in quick successive motions, but the hermit was gone. I clapped the sand off my hands and got to my feet. Just as I lifted my head—that was the infinitesimal fraction of a second, the flash of the moment—I thought I saw my bag vanishing behind a boulder. It was harnessed to a half-crouched, suspicious-looking man.

I shuffled to the giant rock. My bag was gone. *Is this my imagination running wild?* Then it reappeared from the back of another boulder with the thief. *Take immediate cover at first contact with the enemy.* The commander's lesson instinctively resurfaced. I dashed behind the boulder, ducked my head, and kept still for a few seconds. *No ominous activity.* I raised my head cautiously until I was tall enough to peek over the boulder. I saw my bag darting from one boulder to another, and from one bush to another in rapid movements. *What agility the thief possessed! Observe enemy movement from high ground.* I dropped to the ground completely in a leopard prowl and squirmed my way up the slope, negotiating large protruding tree roots along the way. I saw a tree trunk wide enough to conceal me and I pounced behind it. I had a good line of sight from my cover. My bag appeared to be harnessed to the back of what looked like a half-crouched predator hunting down some prey. *I need to get closer.*

I resumed my prone position and slithered down the slope as quickly and as quietly as I could. As I approached the foot of the slope, I hid behind another natural cover—a huge tree root. I thought I saw the predator looking in my direction. *Employ deception.* I gathered a handful of pebbles and lobbed them as far away as I could and waited motionlessly. *No sign of enemy encroachment.* I dashed across the walking path, did a forward roll, and hid behind a bush. I was so close it was almost impossible to have any sight of the man without being seen. *Advance in stealth.* I slithered from cover to cover until I arrived at the entrance of the vampires' den. I made a quick search for any possible routes he might have taken and found none. I inferred that he must have gone into the cave. *I must be mad to go in.* But I was pretty much mad enough for my bag. I decided to wait behind a boulder by the side of the cave.

Now that the adrenaline had subsided, I felt pulsating pains at my elbows and knees. My undershirt was torn and I had cuts and bruises all over. I allowed myself to convalesce and hoped the man might leave the cave so I could go in. As I waited quietly, I recalled the many times when I'd felt like throwing in the towel with my commander's tough lessons, for I'd found them altogether useless in my mission to seek my identity. I felt grateful that I'd persevered through my disinterest. *One never knows whatever learned today may be of use tomorrow.* I made a silent vow to embrace as many lessons as life may so wish to endow.

I spotted a perfect observation post in an old banyan tree just off the cave's direct vision. I snaked through the labyrinth of thick foliage and lay stealthily on a branch, which was as sturdy as a trunk. I fixed my eyes on the cave entrance and waited with controlled breaths. I finally caught sight of the predator, the thief who stole my bag.

*

14

BARNETT HELD A PISTOL in one hand, a whiskey bottle in the other. The moonlight revealed a forlorn profile never before seen on this flamboyant man. Everything he wore was a mess. His signature peacock crest had collapsed into a messy heap of hay; his head hung like a dead pendulum, detached from time, devoid of function.

"Mr. Governor?" Ahiga waved a hand in front of Barnett's drifted eyes. "Sir?"

"Commander..." Barnett grunted without looking at his visitor, "sir."

"What do you have in your hand?" Ahiga queried.

Barnett showed him the whiskey bottle.

"The other hand, I mean."

"Molan's gift."

Molan's gift? Ahiga mused as he stared at the gun in Barnett's quivering hand. "Please, Governor Barnett." He opened his hand to claim the weapon.

Barnett slowly lifted the pistol, jolting the warriors in the truck to full alert.

"Easy," Ahiga coaxed.

Barnett turned the barrel away from Ahiga and dropped

the gun into his hand, much to the warriors' relief. They slouched back into their seats.

Ahiga examined the weapon in his hand. "Firing away into the night, hey? What is this all about?"

Barnett raised the bottle to his lips and gulped the whiskey. "What is this about? This is all about Ahio's people, and my failure as their governor." He took another gulp. "Look at our school…" he moaned, "children with jobless parents have dropped out because they cannot afford even the dinky fee. Look at our hospital—our medical supplies are low. I was told some patients have died due to insufficient medication. Look at our bridges—old and coming apart, and new ones are needed; but Logistics would not lift a finger because the funds are not coming through. Look at our markets—supplies are piling up and being thrown into the garbage because at least a third of our people cut down on living expenses. Look at our sanitation—the shores are awash with sewage. I was told Environment has cut back on workers due to insufficient funds. Look at your barracks—outdated inventory, outdated rations, and outdated"—he cast an emphatic finger at the gun in Ahiga's hand—"armory.

"Why?" he dramatically punctuated his litany of woes.

"Why?" Ahiga rebutted. "Ask yourself: what have you done? What have you been doing all these months? Did we not agree at the tree house to come together for the people? I heard you've been hiding yourself in that glorious white elephant"—he pointed at the sugar mill in the distance, which Barnett had turned into the governor's quarters since his commission—"while your so-called civil servants—but really sugarcane harvesters, choppers, grinders, and millers— sip sweet coffee and tea under the comfort of your ornamental trees. They're all but salaried by national funds!"

He pointed to Barnett's sunken chest. "You are damned right, Barnett. You have failed to govern. You have failed our king and our people." And he challenged the drunkard, "What are you going to do about it?"

Barnett indifferently parried away the prudish finger. "Yes, I have failed. Big time. And I have failed, above all, to have stood by my belief instead of obeying the king's will. Burn every stalk of sugarcane to protect the innocent lives of our people? Look what all this amounts to! Look!" He opened his helpless arms and swirled his body to the imaginary rhythm of a mournful waltz. He turned his body this way to acres of bare space where a plantation once stood, and that way to a row of rundown cottages where hordes of workers used to rest and rejuvenate. "Had I stood firm, all this would not have happened." He gazed into Ahiga's eyes. "*This* is my biggest failure." He took another gulp of numbing whiskey and said resignedly, "The people's needs are inflating, and our money? Deflating. What am I going to do—you ask me?" He cast an accusatory glance at Ahiga. "What can I do? What with the king's will. What with the sugar plantation razed to ashes. What with the pathetic fund that's left!

"'No sugar, no war'? No sugar, no peace!" Barnett concluded.

Ahiga's eyes betrayed a mix of rage and guilt. He was enraged by the drunkard's outright defiance of the king's edict, which he had taken to be infallible. By the same token, he felt guilty for swaying with Barnett's compelling argument against his king. He kept still, retaining a dignified posture. Then he leveled the weapon at Barnett's face. "You were saying—a gift from Molan?"

Barnett jabbed a finger repeatedly at the pistol. "A threat in the guise of a gift, really. The mad dog is flexing her muscles in our face—in your face—Commander!"

Ahiga felt a flush rising to his face. Molan was that one archenemy he had because she was his king's archenemy. Barnett knew the warrior's weak point. He arched his brows and whispered, "I've heard she recently made a tidy investment in that." He pointed menacingly at the gun in Ahiga's clutched hand. He laid his cold gentle hand on the warrior's shoulder, and said, "What am I going to do, you ask? Isn't this a security issue? Commander, sir, what are *you* going to do about this?"

*

WHAT EXACTLY HAS *the old fox crafted? The island falling apart, the financial depletion, the gunshots in the night, Molan's "gift," the arson, and the king's death—which until now has remained unsolved—are they all part of your plot, Barnett? What's your motivation? To usurp every power there is? To gain full control over the island? To garner fame and fortune? Is this a trap I've fallen into? What do you want from me? What's your play, O crafty Barnett?* Ahiga rattled away in his tortured mind.

He had questioned Barnett about the arson, but the onus to undo its dire outcome had somehow—through Barnett's sleight of hand—befallen him. He had confronted Barnett about his irresponsibility, but the governor had thrown the ball back into his court. *Commander, sir, what are you going to do?* His mind echoed Barnett's haunting question. He muttered to himself, in irony, in agony, "What am I to do?" *Tell the governor I need ordnance reinforcement? Does that not amount to asking for money from him? Then what? He had made it clear our finances are in steep decline. What does he want?* Ahiga looped his queries over and over again, until he finally said aloud, "I need help."

"I'm afraid I'm here with more trouble," René's husky voice entered dreadfully. "I knocked, but you were deep in thought," he apologized. "I'm afraid you'll have to come and see for yourself—now." His voice was rid of the usual serenity.

Ahiga replied emotionlessly, numbed as he was by

problems: "With or without troops?"

"They may be useful," said René.

"Five men, now!" the commander ordered his guards.

"Fifty?" René whispered.

"Wrong—five-zero men!" the commander thundered after the guards.

*

A RIOT OF MEN, WOMEN, AND YOUTH crowded the open field outside the King's Assembly House where their king had spoken to them before his fateful voyage. They hoisted placards and banners that bled with the ink of angry sentiments: "Give me back my child!" "Give me back my money!" "Give me back my job!" "Give us a king!" "Down with the French bloodsucker!"—a blood-red X splashed across René's portrait. "Down with aged warriors!"—a big *R.I.P.* splattered over Ahiga's portrait. Mostly, they were Barnett's portraits that bore a range of headings from "Down with Self-serving Leadership!" to "Down with Corruption!" to "Down with the Demon!" The riotous congregation was roaring unstoppably, "Give us a king or give us a boat!"

In the sea beyond the field, a fleet of boats had assembled. Men were seen lugging cartons of food and clothing, and women with infants fastened to them were loaded up. Many of the boats had already sailed off into the Pacific in search of a new king, a new queen, a new leader; some headed northward to the Isle of Molan, Ahio's archenemy.

Barnett stood alone on a makeshift platform facing the riot. His suit was smeared with paint, raw eggs, and rotten tomatoes; his head had been gashed by a hurled rock and was bleeding on the side; his hand was holding the king's scepter. He knew that no language could quell the brewing sentiments better than that which was physically said. Blood was a necessary device. Real blood.

René had scribbled the governor's speech on his way to the scene. Ahiga sent an undercover messenger to slip into the riot and relay the script safely into Barnett's hand. The commander and his company of warriors watched over the crowd from a distant post so as not to arouse their furor with the sight of authority. René, on the commander's advice, remained in the truck.

Barnett pounded the scepter against the platform repeatedly. Another rock flew across his face, missing his eye by inches as he dodged it. He resolved secretly not to dodge again to increase the visual impact with more bloodshed. He had used his workers, he had used fire, he had used his friends, and now he would use his own blood. He unfolded the slip from the messenger and belted out his unrehearsed speech:

"Hear, my brothers and sisters. Here—take the scepter of your beloved king!" He instinctively thrust the scepter toward the riotous audience. "Take this if you think you are deserving, if you think you can bring salvation to our people. Our king had entrusted the scepter of leadership" —he hoisted the scepter—"into my hands. Now, come forward to take this if you think you have what it takes to lead Ahio."

He paused and scanned the crowd for anyone with the audacity to violate the king's edict. No one came forward. He continued, "Take the scepter from me if you want, and…and…"—*Damn the Frenchman!* he thought—"and take my life if you must! But take *not* your good fortune, your peace, your progress, your land of rich soil for granted. Take not your life for granted! Stop your unproductive moaning, whining, spitting, and hitting right away. Instead, take up a scepter over your own life, your own happiness, and your own security! Stop wallowing in your fears and pick yourself up!

"The scepter in my hand is no different from the one in yours. You can take up your scepter and conquer your fears, and defend what you love and live for: your wife, your husband, your son, your daughter, your brother or sister, your very own Ahio. Or you can take up your oar and sail far away from this very land that our ancestors built and which now cries out to you to rebuild. Your scepter is in one hand;

your oar"—he waved his script in the direction of the sea—"is in the other. I, Barnett Ahio, to whom King Ahio IV had entrusted governance over you, take before you my scepter to rebuild the land we all love. I will cooperate with the military commander and the counselor for the betterment of our people, and I resolve to restore all the goodness to Ahio Island and advance us into an even better future. I have made my resolution this very day with all my heart and soul. It is now for you—each and every one of you—to make yours. Your scepter or your oar: Which one will you take?"

He pounded the scepter once, so hard that it sent the people into wild, confused palpitations, and with so much conviction that every subversive placard and banner collapsed into silence.

Ahiga and a troop of men marched through the motionless crowd to escort the governor to the military truck.

*

15

THE SKINHEAD EMERGED from the cave and nipped toward the shoreline. Out of instinct, I ducked under the banyan foliage. My sight negotiated through the leaves and found a natural pinhole. He was treading the soft, fine sand with measured strides and his steps were light and nimble. He stopped in the shallow water, and as he bent forward, his head scanned the vicinity. Then he made a few splashes with his hands and hurried back to the cave with a dripping rag, disappearing like a vanishing trail of smoke into the black cave. In a short while, I could hear the vampires' squeaks and flutters exploding and contracting momentarily. *Is this his lunch hour?* I asked myself; and I shuddered, recalling some of the things people said about his "diabolical diet of bats." I could feel my feet being drawn toward the cave, but I held back with all my might. I waited for him to leave, meanwhile entertaining myself so I wouldn't do anything rash. I plucked banyan leaves, crushing and scattering them, creating my own little snowfall around me.

A good hour later, I heard the short burst of squeaks and flutters again coming from the cave. The skinhead reemerged shortly after. I could see that my bag wasn't with him. He leapt for a bunch of roots hanging from the top of the cave and started climbing, as one would a rope, with incredible agility, until he reached the top of the cave entrance. He scaled a stack of rocks and disappeared from sight. I thought this was a good time to raid his den and reclaim my possession. But there were the vampires to reckon with. I hesitated.

The next thing I knew, I was groping in the cave's cold and black interior amid deafening squeaks. *Get out. Perhaps there's nothing in the bag. Perhaps the skinhead's on his way back. Perhaps it's so dark I will not see my bag even if it is at my feet. Perhaps the skinhead feeds on bats and…boys. Perhaps that isn't my bag after all.*

"Stop it," I commanded my frightened head. I strode forward, my hands stretched before me. I smelled vinegar and sour milk, so I knelt to touch the surface of the rocks. *Limestone.* I heard water trickling toward the far end and it got louder as I got farther in. I followed the sound, one cautious step after another. I was walking pretty much on a straight path for what felt like forever. Then I walked into a wall of rocks before me. They felt cold and slimy. My hands guided me along the wall to negotiate a sharp turn, and as the wall straightened again, the darkness gradually lifted. There was a shaft of light coming down at the end of the tunnel, and the trickling had grown into gushing—the squeaks and flutters were now far behind me. I approached the light and arrived at a partially sunlit enclosure about thirty yards high. I'd counted my steps to dispel my fears—2,241, which amounted to nearly one mile.

There was a waterfall cascading at the end of the enclosure, its water pouring into a large turquoise pool in the middle. I felt like I was in another world, paralyzed as it were by paradise. *My bag!* I remembered. My eyes scanned quickly along the walls. There were four separate recesses. I dashed to the first. It was like a veterinarian's theater with rabbits in small wooden cages stacked against the walls and a metal table in the center. A bloodstained rag was dripping from a rack. *Or is this the skinhead's slaughterhouse?* I shook my head to shake off the distraction. I did a quick scan around. *No bag.* I dashed to the second recess: a wooden table, a wooden bench, a couple of soup bowls and plates, and a stove. *Is this where he cooks his bats—and rabbits?* I shook my head hard again. I looked around. *No bag.* I dashed to the third recess: an unlit hurricane lamp hung in the middle, stacks of books were piled up against the wall, a couple of wooden chests, a wooden bed in the corner, and next to it…my bag. I pounced on my possession and unzipped it. *Nothing.* Then I shuffled to the wooden chest and unfastened its hinge. I lifted its heavy lid with two hands. There was nothing but more books. Bigger books. I slammed the lid shut and made for the other

112

chest. I rummaged through its unending contents: a leather journal and a fountain pen clipped to its side, another journal, a bottle of ink, scattered envelopes, paper boxes of photographs, paintbrushes, another bottle of ink, another journal, letters, and letter pads. Right at the bottom, there was a pile of items wrapped in transparent plastic. On one side of the pile there was a small wooden box. I turned the wrapped bundle over and found my photograph staring at me.

I slid my wrapped possessions into my bag, zipped it, and started my first of 2,241 steps back outside, before the resident with an eye on his neck—who fed on bats and rabbits, and possibly, boys—returned to have me for dinner.

*

I WAS BACK IN THE DARK when the vampires' squeaks and flutters burst aloud, followed by echoes of footsteps drawing in my direction. *Lesson one in night tactical movement: squelch your movement and move only when necessary.* I backed against the wall and stooped as low as I could, and took slow, quiet breaths. The intruder was near. I waited, hoping that the steps would somehow divert to another place. I knew by now that there was only one way in and out of the cave. Still I hoped. The footsteps stopped. I drew my breath and held it in. *What if the eye on his neck could see in the darkness?* Afraid that he might hear my thoughts, I blanked out my mind. And waited.

He took one step. I could hear his breath. He took another step, and another. I could feel wisps of hot air jabbing my neck. I wanted to scream. I wanted to run. I needed to breathe. He was motionless. *He is waiting.* I felt as if I were in the sea without air. I applied the underwater technique of exhaling a little at a time to prolong survival; but soon I was out of breath. *He is still waiting.* I felt dizzy, as if I were passing out, and I gasped and choked.

"Who—" he growled.

Create deception. "A dog!" I shouted. *Dogs don't speak, you idiot!* I barked a few times and ran amok in the dark, barking all the while as I did.

"Petrified…fied…fied?" his voice echoed after me in the haunting dark. "I won't bite…bite…bite…."

*

16

THERE WAS MORE to Ahiga's dreams than met the eye. The warrior had thought that his anxieties over the island's infrastructure, economy, and defense would end when his new government began. The anxieties did not go. What plagued him more than the unsettling dreams, however, was the puzzling question Barnett had posed to him: "What are you going to do about this?"

"What am I supposed to do?" Ahiga mumbled his thought.

"Huh?" René replied. He was swaying idly in the hammock on his veranda and puffing his pipe.

Ahiga's mind was a labyrinth of agonizing detail—the talking bridge, the dead weeping infants, and the fiery sea demon; Barnett, with sheer wit, cornering him into an impasse; Barnett firing away into the night; and Barnett setting his own plantation on fire. Yet, by mentally rehearsing his speech over and over again, he recounted each story with clarity to the priest. He alternated between his nightmares and Barnett's drama, sometimes associating the two as if they were authored by the same source.

He continued, "What if Barnett has plans? What if he

wants to capitalize on the king's death? What if he's in cahoots with the tyrant? What if he devised everything from day one—the sinking, the burning, the depleting accounts, the shooting, the riot and the bleeding, and all that feigned despairing? What if all this has nothing to do with Molan? What if he murdered the royal family? What if he sedated the watchman with valerian? What if he intentionally torched his field worker because the murdered man knew his secrets? What if all he wants is money and more money? What if he wants to make use of me?" To which the priest responded with one calm word, prolonging the monosyllable in a sedative baritone, "Huh?"

"What should I do, Father?" the warrior resigned.

René rose and sat on the edge of his hammock. "What if!" he began, lifting his spectacles with one hand and squeezing his eyes with the other. "What-ifs consist of infinite possibilities and permutations." There was a peculiar tone in his voice, which was at once impersonal and personal—he sounded both scholarly and brotherly. "What if Barnett is trying to help? What if he heroically braved the riotous casting of stones? What if he burned his sugar plantation— which is everything he stands and lives for—against his own will to comply with the king's; or if he sacrificed it 'in exchange for innocent lives'? What if his worker's death was in fact an accident? What if he really has the people in his heart and despairs for them? What if he's done everything he could only to find every result failing him and the people? What if he's escaping from pain and numbing himself by drinking? What if, Ahiga, he sees something that you and I don't?"

René stood up from his hammock and reached for Ahiga's head, which was shaking disapprovingly. "Brother, free your mind from panic before you start to think. Still your heart before you steer your head."

Ahiga folded his eyes, as if those words were the Father's valerian.

"You know what the skinhead once told me?" René continued.

Ahiga opened his eyes, showing a mix of perplexity and wonder.

"He said that our dreams reveal to us what our mind wants to avoid—our heart."

Ahiga widened his eyes with surprise over the skinhead's wisdom, and he nodded to say he knew what dreams were. He said, "The broken bridge reveals my anxiety about our infrastructure. The talking infants reveal my anxiety about our economy. And the sea demon reveals my anxiety about our military." He sighed helplessly. "But can I help it? Our island is falling apart, and I'm hard-pressed for solutions."

René shook his head gently. "Your dreams don't direct

you to your people's needs. They direct you to your needs, to you. The root of your anxiety is neither the events nor the people that unsettles you. It is you.

"I'm sure the people would be happy and honored to have a loyal and caring leader like you, Ahiga. But how can you expect to find sound solutions for them when you're plagued by anxiety? You need to trust—"

"Trust who?" Ahiga interjected. "Trust our governor? Trust our tyrannical neighbor?" He shook his head violently.

"Trust yourself," René said, without a hint of judgment, and playfully added, "you must."

"You mean I don't?"

René winked and whispered, "There you go."

Ahiga suddenly realized that all this time, while he had believed himself to be the king's esteemed warrior—sturdily rooted in discipline and fortitude—deep down, he hadn't believed in himself. He dropped his head.

René held it up, and said, "And if you don't trust yourself, you can at least trust the wind that led your fathers to the shores of Ahio and to safety."

"But the same wind might have sunk my lord's vessel, and—"

"And led him to safety, perhaps?"

"Perhaps," Ahiga murmured.

"Perhaps!" René exclaimed. He drew deeply on his pipe

and puffed a dancing chain of smoke rings into the air. Then he quizzed the warrior, "What is the opposite of death?"

"Why—life!" Ahiga replied.

"Birth," René corrected with a smile. "Birth—not life—is the opposite of death. Every natural phenomenon attests to the universal reality that death is not the end of life.

"Everything that seems to stop existing only seems so. Nothing really dies. We merely go through metamorphosis. We change. The inchworm that 'dies' does not stop existing. It lives on as a butterfly. So, too, the seed that 'dies' and births into a plant. And the egg that 'dies' and births into a bird. So too everything else on this planet. For every death, there's birth. And these endless cycles make the prevailing constant: Life."

"What if that does not apply to man?" Ahiga persisted.

"But what are the odds?" René countered. "What if it does?"

"It is far better to live with hope than without," Ahiga conceded.

"And far more logical and mathematical."

René lumbered casually toward his record player, speaking as he did, "Hope is never certain, for a hope 'dies' once it becomes a reality, like the little inchworm that flowers into a butterfly—that's the nature of hope, for better or worse." He swirled to an imaginary tune, faced Ahiga, and continued, "Yet, true certitude comes with hope."

"Really?" Ahiga scoffed. "It seems I can be certain about a lot of things without hope."

"Like how a child can be certain about failing before his test day arrives?"

Ahiga listened without rebuttal.

René continued, "Certainty is one thing. Certitude is another. Just like how surety differs from assuredness. By 'true certitude' I meant the latter—the deep and enduring sense of assuredness that everything in this world will come out good despite the events that suggest otherwise, *especially* when things suggest otherwise. 'True certitude' is a positive attitude, believing that when everything seems doomed, it only seems that way. Is it not true then that one cannot have true certitude without hope?

"Brother, what will happen to the child if he keeps believing that he will fail his test?"

Ahiga shrugged. "He will subsequently fail every test?"

René nodded. "He will eventually despair. Isn't life without a hope quite literally a life that's hope-less?"

"But he may have every valid reason for his certainty," Ahiga returned to René's analogy of the child, "and perhaps avoiding school altogether may save him the heartache of being disappointed?"

René smiled sadly. Then he said, "Perhaps you and I, as

adults, have been disappointed far too much and often to ever dare to hope again.

"Tell me, who in this world would ever reject a prospect as immeasurably joyful as everlasting happiness, say, if it is right before one's very eyes?"

"Not me," Ahiga muttered.

"Not me, either!"

"But what if—"

"What if!" René exclaimed once again.

"So you believe in life after death?"

"More like, birth after death—yes, I do." René appeared to be in doubt afterward; then he continued, "And at times when I lose hope, and I always do"—he winked—"rather than keep fanning those thoughts of despair, fueling them with more 'certain' thoughts of doom, I recourse—with certitude—to God, my Light."

"And God appears right before you with hope?"

René laughed heartily. "Hocus pocus! I'd like to think so! However, it is always through the ordinary and earthy people—and things—around me that Light dispenses itself."

"Such as?"

"Such as you and your unwavering loyalty and love to the king!" René walked toward his pile of records and emerged with "Hilary's Song." "Such as this, too."

The static came on, then the happy tune, then the

elegant voice. The priest offered his hand. "May I?" The warrior clumsily obliged.

*

AHIGA SAT ALL BY HIMSELF on the peak of Mount Ahio, taking in the ocean view and the swaying trees beneath him. He closed his eyes. He felt the Pacific wind caressing his face. He listened to its whistling. It was wind that disrupted Kublai Khan's ambitious campaign against Japan. It was wind that powered boats and ships to distant lands. It was wind that turned Ahio's windmills and powered the sugarcane mill. It was wind that eroded ancient boulders and tunneled them into caves. It was wind that carried and shaped the earth to create breathtaking landforms such as sand dunes. It was wind that carried his Fathers to the safety of Ahio Island. He called to mind René's words. *Trust the wind.* The benevolent and potent wind—its invisible presence could only be witnessed through its effects. Like courage.

It was the wind, too, that brought about catastrophic storms and floods. It was the wind that blinded the African warriors in the desert. It was the wind that stunted the growth of trees along the coasts of Ahio Island. It was the wind that spread the consuming flames across Barnett's plantation. It was the wind, in all likelihood, that sank his lord's vessel. That malicious and potent wind—like fear.

I can choose, he divined. There would always be two sides of the coin. He could choose to see good or evil in things and in people. And he could choose only for himself. The dream, his dream, was after all about him. He had had courage against his foes in the battlefield. It was now time to pit his courage against his own fears in the battlefield between good and evil, between trust and fear. He might not know with certainty the countless possibilities underlying Barnett's action. But he could know his own, and he could trust the wind to carry out the good even if Barnett meant evil. By the "invisible hands" of the wind, good prevails not by eliminating evil, not even by reducing evil, but by transforming the same reality from evil to good: metamorphosis. He thought that if he withheld his anxious judgment and beheld the king's sunken vessel fearlessly, the perceived evil could turn into good in time. He thought he had found the ancient secret of alchemy. He recalled the challenge Barnett issued to him in a sinisterly tone: "Commander, sir, what are you going to do about this?" He already knew the answer.

Ahiga descended Mount Ahio weightlessly anew, as if the wind was carrying him down the long and winding path.

*

17

TO BE SURE, I WAS GUILTY. *But am I condemnable?* In one act of defiance, I had violated the authorities twice; firstly, against the counsel of the priest and the governor to avoid the skinhead, and secondly, against the warrior's command to steer clear of the vampires' den.

I sneaked into my bed after having sprinted all the way from the cave, to the shore, and back to the barracks. I was excited to have reclaimed my prized possession, and rightfully so, I thought. I was even more excited at the prospect of searching through the items to investigate who I am and where I'd come from. I poured everything in the haversack onto my bed, and relished my great achievement. *To think that I'd defied my own fears against darkness, vampires, and the legendary skinhead!* I pushed a few punches into the air. *Yes!* I was glad to have braved it all, as if I'd emerged stronger from a battle.

I approached the spread of evidence as if it was sacred. I knelt beside the bed and studied everything in a broad sweep. *Where shall I begin?* Then, as though I'd seen the procedure from somewhere, I dashed to the kitchen for a pair of tongs, which were incredulously large compared to the little ones investigators used. Having found nothing more appropriate, I returned without further ado to my investigation, and carefully picked up the empty plastic bag—with my incredulously large tongs—that had contained all the items. I turned it this and that way, and I inferred: *waterproofing*. I was definitely sailing before I lost consciousness.

I counted the items sprawled all over my bed, lifting each with my tongs as I did. They were altogether seven:

1. A faded photograph of a woman and next to her, a man cradling a baby.

2. A sealed letter with the initials "SOS" on the envelope.

3. An unsealed letter with the heading: "My Ambition."

4. Two one-way tickets with the imprint "*Socrates*—To Dartsouth; Departing from San Tommasi, Dartnorth."

5. A slab of moldy chocolate bars with a note handwritten on its wrapper: "Bite once when necessary."

6. A filled water bottle with a note handwritten on its side: "Sip once when necessary."

7. A small wooden box.

After tagging each item with a numbered note, I set out to connect the dots. It was clear from the vessel tickets that I had set sail on *Socrates* from Dartnorth all the way to

Dartsouth. I recalled the warrior's *tatami* map of the Pacific and gasped, "Epic." There were two tickets. Which meant that I had been travelling with someone else. I scribbled in my notebook, which the priest had given me:

1. Who was my travel companion?

Items 5 and 6, sealed in a bag, were evident that collectively the haversack was meant as a survival kit to preempt any emergency. The handwritten notes implied instructions from someone other than myself—whoever that might be—who cared enough for me. It was likely the voice of my travel companion, who was most likely the same person who packed the haversack. I made another note:

2. My travel companion cared for me.

The swaddled infant must be me, given that there could be no rationale to having another person's photo in *my* survival kit. Bare minimum, my commander had taught, is the rule of thumb for survival kits. Although not necessarily so, I couldn't help but perceive the photograph as a family portrait. That would also mean that the man who cradled me was potentially my father, and the woman, my mother. I turned the photo over and found a note in identical handwriting to the survival notes. The strokes were melodious but firm:

> Dearest I. D.,
>
> Remember that you were born little, but bright, like a star. So keep shining, as would a star, for a million years.
>
> Love,
> Mom

I was now certain that I was the cradled child. Given the identical handwriting, I could safely assume that it was the same person who wrote on the photograph and the survival notes, and who packed my survival kit. This person was my mother, who most likely was my travel companion.

3. Was <u>my mother</u> my travel companion?
4. Why were we going to Dartsouth?
5. What does I. D. stand for? What is my name? Who am I?

I nipped the open letter with my tongs and brought it closer to me. It read:

<u>*MY AMBITION*—By I. Draconis</u>

My father, my mother says, is Draconis. I have no memory of my father except of how he looked in photos. My mother never talks about him. I asked her once, "Who's my dad?" and she started to cry. I never asked her about him after that because I don't want to see her cry. She told me once that my father had left us for a faraway place when I was much younger. I love movies, and in the movies, when a father or a mother goes to a "faraway place" it means the person has died and gone to heaven. I am not sure if my father has died and that's what made my mother sad when I asked her about him. If he is not dead, I hope to see him someday. I hope to see my father. It is my dream to ride on my father's shoulders someday, like all my friends who have that privilege every day.

There was a star scribbled at the bottom with remarks in red:

V. good! Keep it up! I would like your mom to visit me soon.

I scrawled away in my notebook, feeling like the investigation was making headway:

5b. *D* stands for Draconis.

I reread my writing, which was sounding less and less like a letter, and I wondered aloud, "What is this?" I had a weak impression of the star and the handwriting in red. "A schoolteacher!" I exclaimed. Then I remembered, "Homework!" *But why is this here?* It must be relevant to our voyage for my mother to pack it in the survival kit. The only rationale I could think of was that my companion—most probably my mother—and I were sailing to a "faraway place" to find my father. I struck two lines across point 4 and wrote a new one:

4. We were heading to Dartsouth to find my father. (Is my father in Dartsouth?)

For some reason, I kept holding on to my essay. I reread it and the sentence, "It is my dream to ride on my father's shoulders someday" jumped out at me. My mother, I inferred, was taking me across the ocean to a "faraway place" to have my dream realized. *My mother loves me.* My tears began to trickle. I wiped my eyes and face and said to myself the one instructional word the warrior never failed to dispense throughout my training: "Focus." I added a line beneath point 3:

Who is my mother? Where is she?

I dropped the essay and moved on with the sealed envelope. I picked it up delicately, as it looked like something important and precious. *What does "SOS" mean?* I used a penknife to slash the sealed envelope. I turned it over and a stash of dollar notes fell out with a folded letter. I unfolded the letter—a short note—and read the words that appeared to be written in a hurry:

To whom it may co

Reading this means that my son is in distress. From a mother who loves her son with all her heart and soul—PLEASE HELP HIM in every way possible. This is all that I've got. If this isn't enough, let me return your favor in my nex

Please hel

It was my mother's handwriting. My tears trickled again. *Focus.* I struck two bold lines across points 1, 2, and 3. For sure, she was with me onboard the vessel. The vessel was in distress and she was trying to save me. *Focus.* She had given all her money to ensure my safety. *Focus.* My trickling tears turned into gushes. I dropped my tongs, my queries, my focus. I wept. After a long time, my weeping gave way to sobs. I found myself gazing through my tears at item 7: the wooden box.

*

IT WAS FUN, the apparatus in my hand—a cardboard rolled into a little tube with a brass cap on each end, a glass lens protruding through one of the caps. I thumbed down the tiny brass lever in the middle and a pin of light shone. I turned off the ceiling light and began swirling the pin of light in swordplay movements that I'd learned from the warrior. I felt like a wizard with extraordinary power in my hand. I could see anything in the dark. I pointed the light at the bed and scanned through the spread of evidence: the vessel tickets, the chocolate bars, the water bottle, the family photograph, the unsealed envelope, the essay, and the wooden box. Each item became more starkly present with the magical apparatus, as if a whole new light was shed upon each of them. "The commander will love this," I said, realizing what a remarkable tool this would make to provide focus. I tiptoed across my bunk to the window. I pointed the light at random: a part of a tree here, the back of a barracks guard yonder. I aimed the light into the vast expanse of the night sky and fooled myself into thinking that I had lit up the moon and the stars.

"All lights out!" a commanding voice thundered in my direction. I ducked beneath the ledge and turned off the portable light in my hand. I tiptoed to my bed and returned the magical instrument to the wooden box. It was fun—the apparatus in my hand.

Carefully, I put everything in my haversack and slipped under my blanket. I couldn't sleep. I needed help to pursue my investigation. I could turn to the warrior or the priest; but no, that would mean exposing my act of defiance against them. I wouldn't especially risk solitary confinement from my commander. What would I say if they asked me where I'd found my bag? I thought about the governor, for he seemed carefree and approachable in comparison. But no, for I didn't yet trust him. He was the only one I hadn't lived with. Which left me with only one other option—the skinhead. Besides, he was the one who had found the bag. Knowing where he'd found it might shed a critical light on the proceedings. I slid my head under the blanket and gasped, "No!" But I knew I didn't have another option.

*

18

BARNETT'S LEGS RESTED ON HIS DESK, his fingers drumming its wooden surface. *He will come begging one day—any day—any moment now.* For weeks, it was all that Barnett had done—wait. The island had flooded occasionally. Malaria mosquitoes were breeding. A bridge had collapsed. Some thirty-three patients had died due to lack of medication. Men were unemployed. Women had deserted the markets. Children dropped out of school. Infants were undernourished. Molan was rumored to have prepared for an impending siege. The governor, on the other hand, displayed indifference at council meetings. Daily conferences were kept brief. His civil workers were left uninstructed, fanning flies in the open field where his plantation had once been, or sipping tea and coffee under the shelter of blossoming trees. He was routinely in his office from eight to five, sipping whatever was left of his whiskey bar, puffing his pipe, drumming his work desk with his unfettered hand—waiting.

A panicky messenger wobbled into his room, stammering, "S-s-sir—"

"Ye-ye-yes!" Barnett mimicked. "Stop your damned stammers! Be functional! Now, speak."

"Commander Ahiga and his troops are approaching!" the messenger announced without a hitch.

Barnett dismissed the messenger with one hand in true royal fashion. He beamed from ear to ear and uttered, "Checkmate."

*

AHIGA AND HIS WARRIORS arrived at the door. "Stay here," he ordered. "Yes, sir!" his warriors thundered together. He pounded a few times on Barnett's door and marched in before the governor answered. Barnett was working on what looked like a pile of petitions that had suddenly appeared on his desk. He peered over his glasses and delightfully exclaimed, "The Commander! What a pleasant surprise!" He walked toward the leather couch and gestured for Ahiga to sit with him. "It's been a while. Come, sir"—he pointed at his whiskey bar with a thumb—"drink?"

Ahiga thrust his palms up and remained standing. "Governor, sir. I need firearms," he said matter-of-factly.

More direct and less pathetic than I'd expected. Barnett spilled his empty pockets and said mournfully, "The country's poor; our funds are almost depleted. I'm afraid—"

"I need firearms," Ahiga shot. "What do you need?"

"Let me see…" Barnett rubbed his hands as if there were

a scrumptious feast before him. "Apart from Defense, there've also been petitions for funds from Logistics, Administration, Health, and Transport." He peered at Ahiga from the corner of his eye. "I'm sure you've heard, what with your very remarkable Intelligence.

"Oh, you were asking, what I need. Well, what do you think I need?"

"To get the plantation running again," said Ahiga, his spine straight as ever, his head motionless.

Quicker than I'd thought. "Fantastic idea," Barnett crooned. He continued, "But only half correct. We are not acquiring swords and stones and shields, Commander. We're talking about firearms—guns and ammunition. And we need them quick. Your Intelligence would have informed you about Molan, I'm sure."

Barnett shut his eyes, folding one counting finger after another until his hand clenched in a fist. "I need a plantation"—he opened his hand to show all fingers to Ahiga—"five times the present size." He stole a quick look at Ahiga, who remained stoically straight, and which permitted him to expand on his terms, "To expedite the process, I need competent men"—he jabbed his finger repeatedly at the young warriors outside—"and hardworking boys. And above all," he laid a finger gently on Ahiga's armored vest, "a supervisor who commands respect." He straightened the armor for him and swept imaginary dust off with a waltzing hand. He swirled one full round and opened his arms. "Do we have a deal, Commander, sir?"

"Consider it done," Ahiga said firmly.

Barnett applauded at a dramatically gradual pace, and said, "Very well. A man who deserves all my respect, indeed." He put both hands over his own chest, and bowed. "And so it shall be," he said conclusively.

Ahiga made for the door. He turned to face Barnett before exiting his office, and in an unwavering voice shot at him, "Just a word of caution—do not misappropriate my goodwill and that of my men and countrymen. For I would not hesitate to exercise enforcement in my capacity as Commander-in-Chief, should you so much as—"

"But of course," Barnett crooned. "Why would I—" he ventured to justify. But Ahiga and his troops had marched off toward the charred plantation.

*

BARNETT'S SMILE, which seemed forever starched to his face, collapsed into a frown the moment Ahiga left. He made himself a strong, icy glass of liquor and sprawled on his couch. This was the day he had planned and pined for, for days and nights—compliantly, patiently, painfully. This was the day he got everything he wanted: a plantation five times the size, men, boys, and the king's most loyal subject. But he was worried. There was something about Ahiga's readiness to give in that worried him. What exactly it was he did not know, but he didn't think it was necessary to find out. *I've gotten what I wanted.*

Today he had gotten everything, but he was hit by a deep sense of nothingness and a haunting sense of loneliness caused by something that he could not—and he would not—put a finger on. He gulped down a mouthful of whiskey and hissed with intoxication when the alcohol funneled down his throat. It was comforting. He had one more, and one more, and one more peg of comfort until he finally passed out and fell dead drunk into the governor's chair.

*

19

ARMED WITH A PIN OF RED LIGHT, I slithered into the night. I had smeared the lens of my portable light with red ink to soften the glare. It was a night tactic I'd learned from my commander, and it felt somewhat strange that I had used it against his guards. That was how I'd slipped past the guard posts without losing my way in the dark. The moment I was out of the barracks, I looked ahead beyond my path of light. It was pitch black. And there in the uncertain darkness, the vampires' den stood waiting. My heart palpitated as I inched toward the skinhead's domain. I wondered if this was a good idea, but it was the only time I could evade the commander's watchful eyes. Besides, I hadn't been able to sleep all night.

I stood gasping before the willowed entrance of the cave. The winds howled and the trees rustled. I was focused: I needed to continue my investigation, and that superseded everything else. After I turned off the light, I took a deep breath and trudged into the cave. Midway into the pitch black, I heard a noise from above and I stopped. I felt a warm droplet of liquid on my exposed shoulder. I sampled it with my fingers. It was a bit sticky and there was a certain texture to it—like starched fluid. I cowered in a kneeling position over my fingers and flicked on my pin of light. It was blood red. "Blood?" I gasped, and immediately hushed myself. I looked up to where the droplet might have fallen from, spying an approximate area in the dark. I thought I saw something big—bigger than a bat—hanging from the ceiling of the cave. *Never expose your light in an open space.* I panicked and aimed the light at the hovering creature. The bat-eater, bathed in a reddish hue, growled at the blinding pin of light, "No!"

"No!" I echoed.

I dropped everything and scrambled out of the cave into the open area, my hellish screams piercing through the howling winds and rustling trees.

My attempt to escape failed. The predator dove at me from behind, and I dropped on all fours onto the ground. He cupped my mouth and lifted me under his arm. "Hush, hush!" he said repeatedly and carried me all the way, all 2,241 paces, into his inner sanctuary, before he dropped me to the ground and un-cupped my mouth. The first thing he said relieved me of every fear I had of him, like a magic wand waved in front of my face. It wasn't so much the words but the incredibly gentle note they carried. He said, "I knew you would come back."

*

"EITHER YOU'RE HIGHLY RATIONAL or just gutsy," the skinhead pointed his slender finger at me. He had big eyes that seemed slightly drawn into their sockets, which made him look somewhat sad and gentle and deep—melancholic. His irises were brown and sparkled oddly with life, contrasting against the rest of his profile. His look was penetrative, as if he knew what was on my mind. He had a small hawk nose that wasn't overly pointed, so he looked more humane than predatory, but depending on his expression it could sway either way. His face was clean. His lips were distinct and small.

He continued, "Considering that you screamed for life on both occasions, I think you're rational rather than gutsy." He was pacing to and fro and turned every five to six steps, apparently thinking as he spoke. I caught a glimpse of the eye on the back of his neck, which looked more like it was imprinted. I had thought it was a real eye when Father René first warned me about him. The skinhead sat some distance to my side on the edge of the green, placid lake that faded into gray and then black, and finally disappeared at the foot of the waterfall. He sat cross-legged and turned to face me.

He started my life story based on the items in my bag and whatever he'd heard from me, in the remarkably gentle voice of a motherly father, "You're from San Tommasi, Dartnorth. The vessel tickets, your mother's dollar notes, and your rational nature confirm that."

Is mom in San Tommasi then? Is there a ship back home, sir? I beseeched desperately in my head. *Never interrupt an adult.* I kept silent.

He got up and squatted next to the rest of the evidence, setting a hurricane lantern next to it. He picked up the SOS letter and knelt on one knee next to me.

"This is an emergency message. Your mother was onboard with you. She wrote this in haste and panic. The ship was going down very fast; that's why she didn't complete her words. She could have packed her bag. She could have run for a lifeboat, or think of ways to save herself. But she did not. She only had one thing on her mind—to get help for you. She packed your survival kit with whatever time she had, and she wrote a note for you in the face of intense adversity, life-threatening adversity." The skinhead reread my mother's SOS note to me, completing her unfinished sentences:

> To whom it may concern—if this isn't enough, let me return your
> favor in my next life—please help…

"She knew. Your mother knew she was going to die, which is why she said she could only repay your benefactor in her 'next life.' If your mother is not found within fourteen days—" the skinhead swayed his head solemnly. "No human being can survive more than fourteen days without fresh water. And it's worse if she had been shedding tears or perspiring. That, and under such treacherous conditions as the Pacific, I'm afraid she's gone. She sacrificed herself for you, and she's gone."

I wept and sobbed uncontrollably. I wailed. I poured out all the grief I had—my longing for a father, for my mother, for my home, all these days on this Godforsaken island, feeling abandoned, banished, punished for nothing I had done that deserved such pain, such grief. "Why?" I howled over and over again until I was breathless and voiceless, and I sobbed in silence.

The skinhead said nothing. He held my head and put me in his bosom. We stayed like that for a long time.

As my sobs subsided, he held my head up and he smiled serenely, the sheen in his brown eyes aglow with sadness, empathy, and respect. "We all have to go someday," he said, "what matters is how we go.

"Your mother gave herself for you, and there's nothing in this world greater than that. Remember the pain, by all means. But remember, too, the love, her love, which will be the light in your world—in our world—in my world, too, so filled with the darkness of despair and the coldness of apathy, hatred, and betrayal.

"Remember her words of truth—'that you were born little, but you are bright, like a star.'" He put the photo down and continued, "In the future, people and the harshness of life may conspire to belittle you, but you must remain as bright and strong as a star that shines for a million years."

He kept ruminatively quiet for a while and muttered to himself, "A star...you're from the north...I. Draconis..." The skinhead suddenly looked excited. "I know your name." He enveloped my hand in his and led me up a wall of boulders, which were naturally staggered into steps. We reached an opening in the ceiling. He pointed to the sky. "That's north." He thrust me up with his slender but powerful arms. "See that tiny, yellowish, twinkling light amid the huge cluster of stars? The only one in yellow, dimmer than the rest?"

I was awed by the expanse of stars, millions upon millions aglow in such splendor I'd never seen. *Focus!* I reminded myself. My eyes explored deep into the cluster to search for the one, yellowish light. *There!* It was flickering weakly among the countless bright, colorless stars, silently but significantly. I nodded, "Yes, yes! I found it!"

The skinhead dropped me to the ground, gasping, "That's Iota Draconis."

*

"IOTA DRACONIS," THE SKINHEAD RELISHED as we

descended from the boulders.

"Yes, sir," I said, proud to have reclaimed my lost identity.

"It's a beautiful star. It's a planet, you know?"

I shook my head.

Then he smiled and exclaimed quietly, "What a beautiful night."

I thought he was weird. *How can it be a beautiful night for anyone who'd just encountered a story as poignant as mine?*

He hesitated, and asked me, "Something to eat, my friend?"

I shuddered and stammered, "Y-y-yes—no! I mean, no thanks."

He smiled as if he knew what was on my mind. "You don't like bats?" He twitched his eyebrows with feigned diabolism. "You'd better hurry back, in that case," he said.

I collected all the items on the floor and dropped them into my haversack. I walked to the skinhead and offered my hand, "Thank you, sir." His warm and tender hand took it, and he said, "Pleasure's all mine, mister."

"So, I am Iota Draconis?" I smiled.

He shook his head approvingly and said, "Beauty."

"Sir, what's your name?"

He hesitated, and said, "Pahi`umi`umi."

"Pa...mi...Sorry?"

"Pa-hee-oomi-oomi," he enunciated.

"Pa-hee-oomi-oomi," I repeated. "What does that mean?"

He rubbed his head with one hand, mimicking a shaver, and said, "Razor."

"I see," I said. "Pa...hee-oom-mi...oomi. Can I call you Pami?" I sought his eyes for approval.

"Pa-mee...Pa-mee...," he muttered meditatively. Then he shrugged. "Why not."

As I made my way back through the black cave, the squeaks and flutters hovering above me, I was suddenly aware that the "vampires" were a harmless cloud of bats after all. *What*, I pondered, *had corrupted my mind into such folly as fear?*

*

20

THE FARMER'S WEARY EYES gazed through his burnt complexion, examining his blistered hands in the comfort of Barnett's newly refurbished cottage. "Commander!" the farmer's co-worker—face smeared with soil, brows soaked with droplets from hard labor, and hands similarly blistered—reported, "The governor's done his rounds for the day." Ahiga rolled his eyes up steadily to his co-worker and said nothing. "The governor's very pleased with our progress," his deputy concluded and excused himself.

The commander-turned-farmer raised his head slowly and said, "Thank you." His weary eyes followed the deputy through the door into the field. Ahiga saw Barnett in the distance, a glass of golden brew in his hand shimmering in the sweltering sun, and nearby, the workers plugging away. The commander-turned-farmer sighed and dropped his head. He began pinching a dried blister repeatedly, meditatively— he tried not to think about Barnett's apparent jest vis-à-vis the apparent exhaustion of the workers. And then René's words rang aloud in his head once more: *Trust the wind*. The farmer forced himself to his feet, picked up his shovel, and ran after his deputy. "Area Delta!" he hollered. His deputy in turn commanded the band of amphibious warriors resting under the tree; the warriors hauled their shovels and scythes as they would their swords and spears—and soon, shotguns and rifles—and double-timed it to Area Delta.

Commander Ahiga divided his field into four key sectors—Alpha, Bravo, Charlie, and Delta—and deployed his men into four corresponding missions. Infantry ploughed Area Alpha soil into fine, even particles in preparation for planting. Swordsmen chopped hundreds of thousands of mature sugarcane stalks into setts concurrently. Amphibious warriors furrowed the ploughed soil and dropped the setts in equal distances once the ploughmen advanced to Area Bravo. A second, smaller troop of amphibious warriors followed to bury the setts and scatter fertilizer. And the navy collected enormous amounts of water from the sea every day for desalination and irrigation.

Ahiga and his troops had built five desalination cylinders from René's illustrated plan. The concept was to heat seawater in the lower chambers, which would evaporate and condense in the upper cool chamber, after which the distilled water would funnel into smaller drums for watering. The navy transported the drums to the plantation every day.

The workforce chain would repeat until all four sectors were ploughed, planted, furrowed and fertilized, and watered. The amphibious warriors would furrow and plant setts today in the final sector.

For months, the warriors, together with men, boys, and physically sturdier women, had spread all over the acres of land with Ahiga at the helm. The commander and a small group of men would roll up their sleeves to cover gaps—be it to plough, plant, furrow, seed, or water—where necessary. Every so often amid the hard, mundane labor, a water-fight followed by laughter burst out to perk weary hearts and wandering minds. Barnett would peek at the sea of laborers from behind his window curtain and relish his achievement with a peg or two of iced, cold whiskey. He knew the cane would sprout very soon because the fire would have increased the turnover rate of soil nutrients. Sometimes, he baited his daughter to his quarters with candy, so she could play his admiring audience for him. Most of the time, he was alone.

He held up a sheet of paper from his desk with the heading "To Do" and savored his exhaustive list of strikethroughs. He returned the sheet to his desk and, smiling, he scribbled two words: What's next?

*

THE RAIN LASHED AT THE SEA in the blinding light of the sun. The muscled warriors danced in the sun shower. The rain swayed with the vacillating wind, creating rhythmic splatters.

The warriors drummed the bases of their wooden buckets. The splattering rain was like a herd of sheep trudging together—this and that way—at the wind's beck and call. Ahiga waved his shovel effortlessly—this and that way—like a music conductor. The warriors jumped and danced jubilantly in the rain, swaying together to their maestro's command. Area Delta, the last of four plantations, had just been fertilized. Now that they were almost done, everyone—especially the navy—had hoped for the wind to carry the rain and bless their toil. The rain was timely.

Barnett's motorcar rumbled into the party. All of a sudden, the dancers froze, their soaked heads and bodies turned to the intruding vehicle, which choked and died abruptly. Barnett stepped out to a spread umbrella—all dry and incredibly handsome, his peacock crest restored as it was before. He came face-to-face with Ahiga—one dry and handsomely jubilant under an umbrella, the other soaked and tattered in the rain, but equally jubilant.

"I want a new sugar mill, old boy!" the dry one spat his words across the heavy downpour. He turned his body slowly so the butler with the umbrella could catch up. He pointed his dripping finger up toward the towering peak of Mount Ahio. He spat at the ground. And he said, "I want it there."

He had come prepared mentally with every justification for building a mill atop a mountain. *No, it's not about making life difficult for you. It will be a tad inconvenient in terms of transportation, but this will signal to Molan our defiance against her tyranny. This will attract passing vessels to stop and visit at chargeable docking and touring fees, which in turn will expedite your arms purchase. The long road up will be an ideal regime for building your warriors' fitness.* He waited for Ahiga to react.

The soaked warrior-turned-farmer peered across the lashing rain into Barnett's eyes with a haunting indifference, and said emotionlessly, "When do we start?"

"T-t-tomorrow?" Barnett tried to contain his stammer.

"Consider it done." The warrior-turned-farmer-turned-doorman opened the motorcar for the governor. "Please."

Barnett's motorcar choked a few times and rumbled away. Ahiga put his face to the beating rain and raised his arms jubilantly. The dance in the sun shower resumed to the drumming beats of the warriors' empty buckets.

*

21

I LOOKED FORWARD to my next home—Barnett's residence—for three and one reasons. Firstly, of the three men, the governor appeared to be by far the most easy-going and fun and colorful. Secondly, I needn't sneak through the commander's guards anymore if I should want to visit Pami. I imagined the governor to be a lot less restricting than the commander. Thirdly, I might even be open with my guardian about my visits, as I felt him to be an understanding and open man. I never imagined there would be a fourth reason, which in time to come would become my most valued motive.

I was packing my belongings when a voice suddenly pealed through the door: "On guard!" I turned to face a sword flying at me. I grasped it firmly, unsheathed it, stood my stance, and fired back, "On guard!"

"Impressive!" my commander shot. He roared in proud laughter.

"Did you just laugh?" I marveled, as it was the first time I'd seen the warrior laugh. "Sir?" I hastened to add.

My commander zapped his laughter instantly.

I put the sword back into its scabbard and bowed. "Thank you, sir," I said, handing the weapon back to its owner.

"She's yours; keep it—you must," my commander ordered.

"Thank you, thank you, sir," I said gratefully. "My own sword!" I celebrated. I looked at him and said, "Sir…" A gush of words was bubbling in my throat: *Do you know I've discovered my name? I'm Iota Draconis. My mother sacrificed her life for me. My home's San Tommasi. How did I find out? I found my bag. The skinhead had it and I raided the—No, I can't tell him.*

"Young man?" he said.

I shook my head. "Nothing."

"You deserve it, young warrior," he indicated to the sword. His eyes darted swiftly at my luggage and said, "It's still a week to go and you're almost ready. Excited? Can't wait?"

I nodded enthusiastically.

"Come with me," he commanded.

"Yes, sir!"

The commander led me to the barracks' canteen. It was past lunch and there wasn't anyone except us. "Grab your tea," he said.

"Yes, sir."

We sat face-to-face at one end of the long wooden table. I got the sense that he wanted to say something important.

"Young warrior," he said. Then he shook his head and muttered to himself, "If only I knew your name."

I do! I spewed nothing.

"Young warrior, I'm not good at this sort of thing, but I need to caution you about something, about some...one."

He knows about Pami! I suppressed my gasp, so that my breath escaped only through my widened eyes.

"The...the..." my commander stammered, which was rare.

The skinhead from the vampires' den! I clasped desperately to the table's sturdy legs.

"It's about the governor."

I shut my eyes in relief and quickly feigned interest: "The governor?"

"Yes, the governor," he said uncomfortably, as if he was speaking at knifepoint. "Beware of Barnett."

He got me all curious. So I asked, "Why?"

"Don't ask too many questions, young man," he retorted.

"Yes, s-sir," I said. *But I've only asked one.*

"All right, all right," he said. "How shall I put this?" he hesitated. "He might use you."

Use me? What do you mean "he might use me"? But no questions allowed, so I rephrased it into a statement, with a puzzled look and very slow nods, "He...might use me...."

"Yes, he might make you his subject, his servant."

"His...ser...vant...."

"He might make you work for him."

I was profoundly confused. *What's wrong with working for him? Had I not done Father René's dishes? Had I not cleaned your barracks? Had I not also enrolled in your patrolling detail?* I couldn't handle this better than to raise my hand, "Permission to ask questions, sir?"

"Granted."

"What's the difference between working for him and prowl-patrolling for you, sir? I do not understand the notion of 'make use,' sir!"

The warrior ruffled his short streaks of black and grey hair into a mess. "Just...just be careful."

I rest my case. "Yes, sir."

"Dismissed!" He waved a hand repeatedly and rested his forehead on the other hand.

"Yes, sir!"

*

IT WAS ANOTHER NIGHT FILLED with clattering cicadas. I was lullabied by its familiar nature, and my mind was drifting from my confounding dialogue with the commander into the realm of dreams. Just then, I heard a few gentle and deliberate knocks next to me. I saw Pami's face staring at me through my window. *Am I dreaming already?* He tunneled nimbly through the sill and bounced onto my bed, which sprang me to my feet. I screamed, "Pa—"

He cupped his hand over my mouth and stayed motionless until I nodded.

I dropped my voice to a whisper, "Pami?"

"Sorry, but I thought you'd want to know this," he whispered back.

We conversed the whole night in my bunk, at the barracks, strictly in whispers. Talk about night tactical movement.

He whipped out a map, unfolded it, and shone a beam of light on it. "I've got one of those, too!" I said, excited that he, too, owned the magical apparatus. Pami didn't seem the least bothered, his eyes focused on the map. I inferred from his indifference that my flashlight was not quite as "magical" as I'd made it out to be. The map was beautifully hand-drawn in blue, green, and brown, with tiny red dots sprinkled all over.

"You drew this?" I asked.

He nodded indifferently, as if to suggest that he drawing it was not the point.

It's nice, I wanted to say. But I kept mum.

He said slowly and emphatically, "I think I know where your father is."

His hand was at my mouth before I could exclaim my

excitement. "Shhh...."

I nodded.

He released his hand and presented his rationale, pointing to specific red dots on the map as he spoke. "Your vessel tickets were one-way, which means your mother had no intention of returning to San Tommasi, at least not in the near future. She had sailed with you for only one intention: to look for your father and be reunited with him, which explains your essay in the survival kit. I could think of no better reason."

"I know! My father is in Dartsouth!" I interrupted, trying to squelch my excitement at once.

"Not likely. Because if your mother had intended to sail all the way to Dartsouth, then I'm afraid she would have been financially irresponsible, which I doubt she was. You see—the money in the envelope is all that she had, and she wouldn't have had enough to last through the entire voyage. And even if she'd planned to live in austerity, she would have had absolutely nothing left by the time she arrived with you on Dartsouth's shores. So...it's improbable—not entirely impossible—but *highly* improbable that your father is in Dartsouth.

"*Socrates*, I've learned, makes another port of call besides San Tommasi: the Isle of Molan. In the Pacific Triangle—formed by Mikio, Molan, and Ahio—only Molan has a port that can accommodate a vessel as big as *Socrates*. And because the triangular cluster lies midway between Dartnorth and Dartsouth, it makes it a natural port of call for passengers and crew alike to take a sort of breather and for the ship to refuel. Your mother, in all likelihood, had planned to disembark with you at Molan."

I had serious doubts about Pami's theory. "But I thought our tickets specifically said 'Dartsouth'? Wouldn't it be 'Isle of Molan' instead, if that was where we were headed?"

Pami stroked my head and whispered, "Bright. Little wonder you're Iota Draconis." Then he went on to answer my query, "Do you know it costs a lot to print a ticket?"

I shook my head.

"To cut cost, the operators will only print one type of tickets, and only the final destination on them. The handful of passengers who disembark at Molan do not justify the additional cost of making another plate."

It sounded like he made sense even as I hadn't completely understood what he had said. I gathered that the "plate" was some kind of mold from which prints were made, and that it was expensive to make one. I would have pursued the interesting topic of printing had it not been that my mind was currently filled with only one thing. "So my father is in Molan?" I sought.

"Possibly. It could also be Mikio or...Ahio," Pami

suggested.

I wheezed at the third possibility.

"The captain would typically use his lifeboats to ferry passengers to neighboring islands. Those who sought entertainment and recreation would be ferried to Mikio. Those wearied souls who pined for an idyllic rest stop would be ferried to Ahio.

"*Socrates*, as far as I know, had not made its port of call. It was wrecked before arriving in Molan."

I re-examined the distance between north of Molan, where the vessel allegedly wrecked, and Ahio, where I was found. "I must have drifted a long way. Is that even possible?"

Pami shook his head. "You would not have survived. Every vessel must avoid the passage north of Molan because of the dense rocks on the seabed. Ships must head south, passing through the western passage of Molan before detouring back up north to dock at its southern cape." He pointed at the biggest red dot on the map, a spot north of Ahio and south of Molan. "I think it was here where a powerful easterly crashed into your ship while it was making a portside turn toward Molan. This was where the shipwreck took place.

"It all adds up. I am sure that *Socrates* was wrecked on its way to Molan, where your mother had planned to disembark, either to find your father there or in equal probability, Mikio or…here. Iota…"

"Yes." I held my breath.

"Your father could be closer to you than you think!" It was his turn to suppress the excitement in his voice.

I nodded enthusiastically.

"Your father could be any of the men in Ahio."

*

I RANSACKED my mind for clues. Pami had left me with hope, and I felt that my dream to be carried on my pa's shoulders would soon be realized. It could be anyone. It could be Father René, Commander Ahiga, or Governor Barnett. It could be one of the infantry or navy warriors, one of the guards I slipped past in the night, or the cook, the driver, the swordsman, or one of the governor's thousands of workmen. It could also be Pami. I would rule no one out. I thought of a way to shortlist my suspects—to find out who among them had been to San Tommasi: where my mother was and where I had been born.

*

22

PAHI‘UMI‘UMI LAY QUIETLY in the tree, his contemplative eyes affixed to his old home—the tree house in the banyan. There was something about the tree house that drew him in its direction. It was his private meeting with the king, the significance of which he hadn't forgotten. In the next moment, he found himself gazing at his house with a mix of nostalgia and sadness and sense of glory from the inside. He reminisced about the day before Ahio IV delivered his farewell speech to the people. This was where they had met in secret.

The king had shed his robe and sought the skinhead's audience in private. He was alone, without his usual entourage of guards, butlers, and navy warriors. "Are you there, Umi?" the king had whispered unbecomingly at the door.

The skinhead opened the door and genuflected. "Your Highness"—he showed the king in—"how can I be of service to you today?"

Without delay, the king recounted to the skinhead the details of Queen Molan's dubious invitation and disclosed his strategies.

"Plan A is to launch an offensive campaign. I'm confident that Ahiga and his warriors can take on Molan's anytime. Due to the open seas between our islands, Molan's watchmen could see our encroachment clearly, which is why I'm considering a night assault, where visibility is minimal. To further conceal ourselves, our troops will wait in the distance for the pre-dawn fog before landing. The fog is ninety-percent affirmative. I've heard the French priest's meteorological prediction. He ascertained that in the next few days a chilly pre-dawn northwesterly would meet the seawater surface, which for days has been warmed tremendously by the cloudless sky—making it perfect for heavy fogging. Once the troops have landed, they will launch a swift, surprise assault centralized on the barracks. Molan will be crippled—no, paralyzed—without her commander. A centralized assault will also protect innocent civilians from unnecessary bloodshed and death." The king paused for the advisor to digest his plan, and then permitted him to speak by silently meeting his eyes.

"How sure are we of Molan's intent?" the advisor asked.

"Fifty-fifty at best," the king replied.

Pahi`umi`umi nodded contemplatively. "What's next after Ahiga captures Molan's force?"

"Unification," the king hastened, adding, "under one rule—our rule."

"We will subject Queen Molan to our dynasty?"

The king nodded.

"And if she doesn't comply, we'll execute her along with those who refuse us?"

The king replied, "So it shall be."

"Your Highness, that will not work. We'll be sending an unfriendly signal to Mikio, and every ally in the Pacific—worst of all, to Dartnorth and Dartsouth. These two heavyweights will boycott our economy. The Ahios have never been known as an offensive tribe, but as a friend to all. This will change everything. We would have no chance to justify our act of violence—a surprise and night offense, at that. We'll be seen as a tyrannical and sinister force to be dealt with. We are as good as severing all friendly ties with our neighbors, and we can forget about forging new ones. It's a move that will inevitably lead us to self-annihilation.

"Unless of course we have ample evidence against Molan's impending threat; which we don't, save for our fifty-fifty speculation, which hardly suffices in justifying any act of war. This is criminal."

There was something final in the skinhead's tone when he pronounced the last three words. It was as if they were spoken with the king's authority, the king's voice.

"Plan B, Your Highness?" The skinhead knew he had compellingly deterred the king when the sovereign sank his head into his own hands.

The king looked up, trying to regain focus, and dispensed Plan B, his kingly tone restored once again: "Another plan is to devise a fictionalized plot to turn down Molan's invitation without incurring her wrath. The king or the queen is engaged in some crucial matter, the royalty is obliged to remain on the island; the king is sickly; the queen is unwell; the vessel is unfit; and so on. And we profoundly regret turning down your desirable invitation and we wish the princess and her new prince every happiness. Or we can—"

The skinhead interrupted the king, "Whatever story and however convincing, this, Your Highness, is an act of cowardice, no matter how you say it. I suppose that you have every intention of hiding the truth from your people?"

The king nodded reluctantly.

"May I speak bluntly, Your Highness?"

The king nodded; again, reluctantly.

"You can hide from your people, even from the world, but you cannot hide from yourself, Your Highness. You will live the rest of your kingly life with a lie you have concocted out of your own fear. Can you accept this? Can you, if I may ask, still live with true royal dignity every time a subject bows to you in true reverence?"

The king shook his head.

"I didn't think so. I can't vouch for anyone else but you.

I remember when we were children and we were in the woods. You picked up an injured bird and you held it tenderly in your hands and you bit your own tongue and you snapped the bird's neck into two. I asked you why. And you told me something I've never forgotten. You said, 'Being good is not the same as being nice.' You'd gone against your sentiments and freed the bird from pain and misery. Such is the courage and compassion that makes you a great king, a great person. Such is the hero that I know you to be. I've never known you to be cowardly, and I believe that you are not.

"Let's just say we bypass our heroic conscience; let's just say the whole 'hero' idea is just too outlandish and impractical. Let's just assume that we are not cowering from Molan's challenge, and that staying alive is a purely pragmatic act of self-preservation. Let's just convince ourselves—how I do not know—that we are not in fact afraid, but being practical in evading Molan's 'challenge.' Even so, Your Highness, you can trust the tyrant to effectively expose your cowardice to the world, and to your people. Of this, I'm one hundred percent sure.

"To give Molan the chance to undermine you is detestable. But to allow Molan to witness your weakness is disastrous. That will open our gates for an assault, even if she did not plan one."

The king was speechless and lost.

Pahi`umi`umi rose and paced about in the tree house, thinking very hard, for his king was awaiting a solution to end the agony. Then he approached the king, and held him with a penetrative look; and he said, "This is the moment. This is the moment that separates one king from another. There are kings who compel their subjects to their knees by force and all kinds of suppressive measures; and there are those who do so by virtue of who they are: kings, true kings. This isn't a moral issue, so there's neither 'wrong' nor 'evil.' This is a matter of choice. This is a matter of preference. This is purely a matter of what you really desire. Period.

"There is only one way to do this if you want to be a true king: to rise to Molan's challenge of an invitation. To meet her as a true king would. What do you desire?"

The king said nothing. The two men remained in silence, as if enveloped in profound reverence by the moment, for the moment; as if the matter at hand was a matter of sacredness.

The skinhead broke the silence, "Your Highness?"

The king looked up wearily.

The skinhead tried to soften the tension for him, "You do have a choice, Your Highness. You are free to choose."

The king nodded.

"There is no 'wrong' in this situation. To preserve one's own life even if you must resort to lies is a right thing to do, insofar as self-preservation constitutes a basic tenet of Natural

Law. To rise to Molan's challenge, which means putting your life and the royal family's at a fifty-fifty risk—for the love and dignity of your people and yourself—is the great thing to do. So take heart, my lord. You are either right or great."

"I'm...afraid," the king crumbled.

The skinhead said nothing further; he already knew the king's decision. He shut his eyes empathetically. He felt the king's turmoil for a while. He gathered himself, and said, "Who isn't?"

He retreated to his writing desk in the corner, while the king rose quietly and walked to the window. The king looked at the leaves swaying compliantly in the wind. It gave him a sense of calm. Then he looked at the huge and deeply rooted banyan trunk. It gave him strength. He stood by the window in silence and let nature restore his sovereign disposition.

The skinhead returned from his desk with two enclosed writings, one titled "To My People," the other "To the Fathers of Ahio." He said, "The first one is your speech to the people; the other one is the king's will addressed to Ahiga, Barnett, and René."

The king received them with a mix of fear and gratitude. As he departed from the little tree house, Pahi`umi`umi said to him, "I will sail with you."

*

23

IN SPITE OF THE ACHING QUERIES that enmeshed my heart, I was in love—if being in love means liking someone affectionately. She was the world's most beautiful girl. She was as exotic as any native I'd met, and that, coupled with her big green eyes, was enough to hold me spellbound. We hadn't even begun to speak.

After tossing my sword and books and other collectibles, such as pebbles, rocks, and leaves, and my clothes—which were minimal—onto the back of his truck, my commander shoved me into the front, and we made for San Tommaso. For some reason, he was befuddled that the governor had specifically instructed me to meet him there. He kept mumbling as he drove, "What is he up to?" and "What now, Barnett?" Me, I had only one thing on my mind the minute he mentioned, "San Tommaso."

My voice jumped along with the bumpy ride, "Sir, why is the Father's school called 'San Tommaso'?" He shrugged, looking preoccupied with something else. "Do you know where San Tommasi is?" I pressed on. "Is San Tommasi the same as San Tommaso? Has Father René been to San Tommasi? Is that why he stays in San Tommaso? Is that why he named it San Tommaso? Did he name the school?" *Does he know my mother? Did my mother have me with him? Is he my father?* Of course, I forced the last three questions back to my gut before they gushed out of my otherwise unstoppable mouth.

He stared at me blankly, as if I were some babbling alien, seemingly more disturbed than when we had left the barracks. "That was close!" he exclaimed all of a sudden, swerving the truck sharply and missing a boulder by the road by a few inches. I decided to let him drive.

The truck passed the old banyan tree from where I had espied Pami's predatory profile for the first time. He had shuttled like a shadow between the sea and the cave, a rag soaked in seawater and blood dripping from his beastly hand. I chuckled aloud, much to my commander's surprise. "Nothing," I said, rather defensively, as he hadn't said a thing. I was laughing at how one's mind—my mind—could actually scare oneself into such baseless suspicions.

My mind went along with Pami, and I snickered once more, recalling my first dinner with him. He had invited me to his cave with a note he had sneaked through the barracks, into my bunk, and onto my desk: "I've made dinner. Come tonight." I was deep into the cave when a sudden awakening turned my enthusiasm into concern. *Dinner? What was I thinking? He feeds on bats and rabbits!* But by then Pami had heard my footsteps; it was too late to change my mind. The next thing I knew, he'd sat me in front of a boiling pot.

"What's this?" I pointed to the stew.

"Stew," Pami replied matter-of-factly.

Stew? Rabbit stew? Bat stew? Apply delay tactic when in doubt. I lifted the spoonful of God-knows-what to my mouth in super-slow motion. *Think, think!* Then I dropped the spoon back abruptly.

"What's wrong?" he asked, although his eyes suggested he read my mind.

"Were you running after," I ventured, and motioned my head toward his slaughter room, "a rabbit?"

He craned his omniscient head near mine, and said softly, "Why, all the time!" Then he burst into laughter. "One of my hobbies is hunting down injured rabbits," he said, disclosing to me his noble passion for nursing them, which relieved me from the suspicion that my dinner was going to be a rabbit, which also implied—to my horror—that dinner was bat stew.

I lifted my elbows and hesitantly flapped my hands at my sides. "Is this a b—"

"Beef," he bellowed with finality.

I wasn't convinced because I clearly saw him with my own eyes feeding the bats just days ago. I shot at point-blank, "Sir, what were you doing at the cave's ceiling, dripping with blood?"

"Experimentation," he said, seemingly annoyed that I was disrupting his dinner. He looked at me, then at the cutlery in my motionless hands, and he laughed, shaking his head helplessly, and giving in to my inquisition: "I don't feed on bats. I just feed on knowledge—in this case, to find out if the fruit-eaters would nip the fresh meat from my hand."

"Fresh *meat*, did you say, sir?"

Pami rolled his eyes up. "Fresh *chicken* meat."

I devoured the beef stew and asked for another helping.

*

THE TRUCK SCREECHED TO A HALT. Father René walked toward us with open arms. "My child!" his words at first lobbed lightly into the air, then raced excitedly into my heart.

"My father!" I said in a slip.

He laughed as we hugged. "How's the young warrior doing?" He thrust me away to examine my built body. "A young warrior, indeed!" he remarked at my commander, who still looked perturbed.

"What is he up to?" my commander said discreetly, as he pulled the Father aside.

The Father looked at me and said, "Young warrior, grab your stuff and wait in the refectory." He looked up at the sky and squinted at the sun. "Grab yourself something cold while you're at it, all right?"

I nodded. The two men immediately engaged in whispers.

I lugged my belongings from the truck and made for my icy drink, my mind filled with the possibility that the old man I just embraced was my father. *Why else would he be the first and only person at my side when I came to from my concussion? Why else would he specifically instruct me to address him as "Father"? Why else would he chase after me, almost crippling himself in the process? He did not even ask for my name! Because he knows who I am! Is it any wonder that his school is named after my mother's home? And yes! His eyes are blue—like mine—like no one else's on this island. Why else would he—*

My mind froze all of a sudden. My heart palpitated once again, but this time for an entirely different reason. It was the most beautiful pair of eyes I'd ever seen, and they were looking at me. And the owner was smiling at me. I dropped my luggage instantly, and along with that, my jaw. She waved with one hand and said, "Hello, I'm Chloe." And she extended her little hand to make acquaintance with me. I extended mine, unsurely.

And I am Iota Draconis, the star from the northern hemisphere, the one and only! But nothing came out of my nervous lips, save this: "I...I...I..." I pointed to the fridge in the kitchen to escape my embarrassment, and finished my introduction with incoherence, "I…Lemonade!"

I wanted to shake her hand, to kiss her hand as any fine gentleman would, but I brushed it hastily and galloped away like a defeated stallion—no, a cowardly pony—into the kitchen. I fumbled for a glass, for the fridge, for ice, for my lemonade, my head locked to the front.

"Lemonade? Nice name!" she snickered at my back.

I slugged down my lemonade, facing the fridge as if there was something in it that held great importance. I turned around clumsily and hastened, "Excuse me," brushing her side and dashing off to…to…*Ah!* To my sword!

She was sitting alone at the dining table when I returned with my sword, her chin resting restlessly on her hands, her idle legs kicking the air beneath.

"See!" I held out my mighty sword.

"That's nice," she patronized, and said, "My dad has a gun!"

Plan B! Plan B! Quick, think! There being no other plans, I conceded with a wimpy, "Wow!" Then I sat across from her, looking in every direction except at her. The silence between us was awkward, so I initiated a conversation. "Do I know your dad?" I asked, which made me feel even more awkward because the question came after a five-minute lag.

"I would think so," she said in a tone mixed with confidence and indifference. "Everyone knows him. He's the governor."

I wanted to dash into the kitchen for another serving of lemonade, which I did. I came back with the clattering glass, this time avowed to stay composed at all costs. "What does the governor do exactly?" I tried to sound profound.

She shrugged indifferently. She looked at her watch—which seemed too incredibly big for her little hand—and frowned, "He's late again."

"That's all right," I said in a manner as gentlemanly as I could possibly pull off. "We can always make love—I mean make up—for lost time." *Nice, second slip of the day in no more than twenty minutes.*

"I guess," she frowned again.

I tried to cheer her up and impress her. I showed her my pebble collection. I showed her rocks. I showed her the dead plants I'd collected, to which she surprisingly responded with keenness.

"What's that?" she pointed at a dried flower with her slender finger.

I cleared my throat rather dramatically. "This? This is a Golden Candle, so-called because its flowers are shaped and colored like one. They're beautiful!" I scattered all the plants I had all over the table, and said proudly, "I have one for every letter of the alphabet from A to Z."

Her eyes glowed.

I presented my collection to the princess one by one: "allamanda; bird of paradise; candlenut; dogtail; emilia—be careful, it's prickly; fireball—its flowers are beautiful, like a fireball; golden candle—you've got that already; hanging lobster claws; indianhead ginger—not exactly a ginger; jumbie bean—I can make you a nice necklace from its beans someday; Koster's curse; little bell; miracle leaf; nun's orchid; ox eye—a kind of daisy; parrot's beak; queen of the night—a night-blooming jasmine actually; rosary pea; sea grape—I got all wet for that; temple tree—frangipani, actually; umbrella tree; velvetberry—tiny blue flowers; white lady—its flower opens up in splendor like a lady in white; yellow oleander; and last but not least, I give you zingiber zerumbet."

She covered her lips and chuckled, "Did you make that last one up?"

"No, it's actually better known as wild ginger; but I needed a Z."

"And you need an X, too."

I wondered for a moment, a wishful moment, if she was asking to kiss me. *Focus, focus!* I shrugged and told her, "Yes, I need an X, but not a single hope in the whole of Ahio, I'm afraid." I instinctively made up for my failure with an exploratory spirit, "Maybe someday I'll sail faraway to complete my collection."

She reexamined the sprawled collectibles on the table and

she clapped. The daintiness with which she applauded sent my heart throbbing away. "How do you know so much?" she asked.

"Father. *René*." I replied.

"Talking behind my back, I see," the Father's husky voice came from the door.

We both laughed.

The governor came in after him with my commander. "You're sooo late!" Chloe taunted.

"Sorry, my darling," the governor knelt next to his daughter and pecked her forehead. He turned to me. "Seems like you guys hit it off. That's great! I was afraid—"

"His name is Lemonade," Chloe interrupted.

The governor laughed. "Nice name!" He rustled my head. "Shall we?" And he took the sword from me. "Allow me." The gentlemanly governor turned to Father René, and then to Commander Ahiga, dipping his head at each of my previous guardians. "Gentlemen."

"Governor, sir," the Father repaid his courtesy. My commander nodded emotionlessly. I thought I saw him cast a suspicious glare at my new guardian.

*

24

PAHI`UMI`UMI HAD IMMENSE POWER not seen from the outside. His tree house was built with columns of oak trunks bound to each other. The solid trunks were hauled, singlehandedly, on his small but very strong shoulder to where they now stood. Save for an altered layout inside, the tree house on the banyan hadn't changed much. The white interior remained a contrast to its bark exterior mottled with moss. The builder had kept the bark on the exterior as a protective layer against weathering and pared the trunks on the inside for a brighter, cleaner, and more appealing interior. Pahi`umi`umi sat on a solid stool, which he had crafted from one of the bigger trunks, as he reminisced about the secret encounter he had had with the king. He listened to the birds and the leaves, and the quiet nature of the forest. Then he heard the tightening of ropes, followed by voices, half-laughter, and heaving sighs. *Someone's coming!* He rose instantly and made for the window. He swung his legs up onto the ledge and thrust his inverted body over the thatched roof, where he remained motionless. Ahiga, Barnett, and René walked into the tree house, missing him by seconds.

Ahiga put a finger to his lips and squirreled to the

window. He jigged his head through and looked up. Nothing. The other two men doddered to their oak stools to recover from the rope climb.

René heaved, slugging air between words, "To think that the skinhead used to do this several times a day—I must say the man is quite something." Barnett hung his jacket over an intruding tree branch and rummaged in his pocket. His hand emerged with an aluminum whiskey flask toward which René extended a wobbling hand.

Ahiga stood at the window, his locked spine as straight as ever. "I officially ordered my prowlers to keep their eyes open for any clue of his presence. Is it any wonder that the man disappeared right after the king's passing? I would take no chances. If it is true that he's lurking somewhere—in the woods or in the cave—he must be up to something. I know from the port annals that the skinhead has made a total of three hundred and twenty trips to the Isle of Molan in the last ten years—all under the name of Pahi`umi`umi. This man is a potential threat. Keep a close watch on him—we must. I don't want anyone on our island slashed in any way by the 'Razor.'"

René hissed from the alcohol kick, reinvigorated. "Ahiga," he said, "you and your queer taste for rats—you keep smelling them, don't you? I've had several tea sessions with the skinhead—in my school and, sometimes, over here." He pointed firmly to the planked flooring. "Let me tell you what I know about this man. In one word: mystery. Two words: deep mystery. He's the most elusive person I've met since the time I left my home in France. What can you say about mystery if not that it is unknowable? But this much I know— he's a man of heroic values and incisive wisdom. You want to talk about smelling a rat? This man can truly perceive a rat for miles—and not from sheer paranoia!" He tossed a playful look at Ahiga. "From my many conversations with him, I gather that he's well-traveled, well-read, and well-cultured, actually, despite his eccentricity, and aloofness, and"—he pointed to the back of his own neck—"rebellious nature. I'm not surprised at all by his frequent visits to the Isle of Molan. Why, he's a man of broad horizons. Besides, he made trips to Mikio as well—if you look at your annals again, Commander.

"As to why he disappeared right after the king's vessel sank, that I don't know. Maybe he loved the king so much he was driven by grief to withdraw from everything that reminded him of the king? Maybe he left for no other reason than to have a bigger, quieter habitat—the cave, perhaps? Or maybe he got sick of climbing the rope ladder? Maybe it's totally unrelated, purely coincidental? Maybe—"

"Maybe he's just"—Barnett drew furious circles at his temple—"a nutcase! Gentlemen, how does all that matter to our future, which we're here to discuss? The skinhead went nuts after the king died, and he's currently on a weird diet of bats. And that's it! No one's going to get hurt, really, save for the"—his interlocked hands flapped in the air—"damned bats! Just as well; they drop feces on my damned canes, I was told." He continued flapping his hands until they hovered outside the window. "No more bats, no more talks about the skinhead please, gentlemen. Can we get on with business?"

*

THE SKINHEAD BURIED HIS HEAD into his hands and pondered the perceptions people had of him: Bat-eater, nutcase, rebellious. *Nutcase? Why not unique? Eccentric? Why not different? Mysterious? Why not mystical? Aloof? Why not self-transcending? Dangerous? Why not truthful?*

He sputtered a burst of self-deprecating laughter and hurriedly cupped his mouth. Then he quieted himself and put his ear back on the thatched roof.

*

"SPEAKING OF the damned canes!" Barnett chortled, and proudly went on with the progress of the new plantation and how the fire had "accidentally" hastened the nutrient turnover. He reported on how within fifteen months the island was quickly resettling to stability with a steady influx of revenue pouring in chiefly from his sugar exports. He looked admirably at Ahiga and extended his hand, to which the warrior-turned-farmer-turned-doorman-turned-house builder obliged. He said, "You have my utmost admiration, sir!" He released his firm grasp of Ahiga's blistered hand and took a bow. "You have far exceeded my expectations. I cannot think of anyone else who can build a house on a hill in fifteen months. Unthinkable. Colossal!"

"Pity"—he shook his head to grieve a great loss— "pity such a huge talent is all cooped up in the damned barracks."

Ahiga smiled and thanked him. Then he switched abruptly to business. "When are my firearms arriving, Governor?"

"Ah!" Barnett pointed to his temple and said, "Underway! I'm on it, Commander. Fret not—if Barnett promises, Barnett delivers!"

It was true. He might not have needed to verbally promise Ahiga the many advantages of having the mill built on the mountain, but they would all come true. The passing vessels would dock and visit for lucrative fees, and Molan would receive a clear signal from her neighbor that it was no pushover despite the fall of the Ahio dynasty. It would all come true soon. Ahiga's warriors had already displayed an improvement in fitness, what with their daily regime on foot up the chastising slope.

It was equally true, however, that the commander's firearms hadn't arrived, and equally true that Barnett had personal plans for the use of this great architectural feat, rivaled by none in the Pacific.

*

25

I HAD UNLIMITED FREEDOM at the Barnett residence. Why? Because Governor Barnett was hardly home. Unlike the commander's barracks, I could do almost anything I wanted here so long as I didn't break anything, and, more importantly, I paid my dues—in kind—to the house owner. I loved the freedom here, even though from time to time I wondered if "freedom" to do what I wanted to do was a good thing.

It was my first night arriving here. I was in the front seat, the governor and his princess—our princess—were in the back of the motorcar. We drove in the dark and it felt like a perpetual climb up, and up, and up, and up. I marveled at the tons upon tons of bricks and mortar, and stones and oak that had been carried strenuously up this punishing road to the pinnacle. As we ascended in the dark, I saw a shaft of light emerging gradually from the hilltop. The light gradually revealed the stunning house, like a grand Victorian curtain hoisting for an epic in the complete darkness of a theater. I watched the steeple rising, and rising, and rising as if it would go on forever. Then I finally saw the roof. *What an incredibly tall steeple! Who stays in there?* I wondered. Then I saw the house, and then the gateway with an overhead arch carved in white: "Barnett Residence."

"Impressed?" the man in the backseat chortled.

I nodded speechlessly.

A troop of ladies and men spilled out of the house to meet whatever needs we had. A few young men—boys—came forward for my luggage and sword. I felt lavishly endowed. Unlike the barracks, where a single worker was piled up with tons of things before he carried them off, over here, I had one each for my bag, my sword, and my collectibles. One of the ladies held my hand and led me into the house. I was greeted by an opulent chandelier that descended from the apex of the endless steeple; the tree of crystals glowed in rainbow chatoyance, casting a constellation of aureoles all over the interior: on the pastel motif walls, gold-framed paintings, and burgundy carpets.

The proud owner of the house swirled around and said cordially, "Make yourself at home." Then he walked a few steps and turned to me again. "And make yourself useful." He said this with cordialness, but with a dramatic emphasis on the last word. I volunteered there and then to chaperon the princess home from San Tommaso on the days when the governor could not deploy his driver. *Am I used, or am I just making the situation useful?*

"Sir!" I called after the owner of this magnum opus.

"Who plays the piano here?" I pointed sheepishly at the white baby grand in the middle of the hall. The man shrugged indifferently and swaggered off. No one, I would learn in days to come, played the piano.

*

NOT THAT I COMPLAINED, but my chaperon service increased from once, to twice, to once every two days a week. We were children with freedom. We were a young couple with private moments. We talked about everything—well, almost everything—under the sun and moon, including the mutual "What's-down-there" and "If-I-let-you-see-mine-will-you-let-me-see-yours" rituals of adolescence. We never kissed. Not that I didn't want to. But we just never did. In hindsight, I revered her too—in this case, healthily—much; and she never made her move, either.

It was Chloe's fifteenth birthday. Her father threw her a soirée. The guests formed a comprehensive list of dignitaries and business associates from neighboring islets and islands, short of the Isle of Molan, and short of Chloe's own friends. I found the big band in the garden a tad noisy, the crowd a tad rowdy, and my birthday girl a tad lonely; so I took the liberty of taking her to a quiet place to celebrate her birthday: my room. I wanted to give her all the attention that birthday girls would normally receive. What with my absent-mindedness, I'd left the secrets from my haversack sprawled all over the bed. It was too late to hide them.

"What are these, your toys?" Chloe's curiosity was seriously aroused.

She wasn't exactly wrong. But to me, it meant something so much more; it meant the epic search for my true father. She sat quietly next to the spread of evidence, darting her eyes curiously between each item.

"Can you keep secrets?" I replied.

"I believe so," she said fleetingly.

I was not convinced. But I thought my story would make an unmatched surprise for her birthday, compared to the wimpy peck that I'd planned on her lovely cheek. I told her everything: the orders I'd received from Father René and my commander to avoid "the skinhead," and how I'd defied them; the glorious day when I raided the vampires' den, the mention of which made her wheeze behind her shocked tiny hands; and the night the skinhead sneaked into my bunk with new findings, informing me of my father's close proximity. And I told her my name. I was delighted that she was the first to know, apart from Pami.

"Who do you think my father could be?" I asked.

"Did the skinhead murder the king?" she replied.

I gathered that certain things interested her more than

others—like sensational scuttlebutts over who my father is. I got the drift. So I played along. I arched my brows to indicate that I had a secret to tell. "Do you want to know what really happened?"

It worked—she nodded religiously.

I whispered, "He was on the king's ship the day it sank!" It was true. Pami had disclosed that to me at one of our dinners.

"What?" She almost jumped up.

"Shhh," I whispered dramatically, "the skinhead said the ship was hit by a powerful, venomous,"—I showed her my fangs and claws— "sea demon," I hissed, "Eurus."

She cowered in my arms. *People tell haunting tales to impress others, for attention, for empowerment*—I added another one to my list of insights, and locked it in the sacred chamber of my mind.

Chloe disengaged from my embrace all of a sudden, her face instantly displayed a haunting expression not unlike my demonic impersonation—she was smiling without any show of emotion. And she said, "Which comes first—the chicken or the egg?"

I felt a tad disturbed that she could switch between two unrelated subjects so quickly, and that she could smile without emotion. But it was her birthday, and the only thing I wanted was for her to be happy. So I just went along with her. I said, "Chicken!"

She rebutted instantly, "But the chicken can't hatch without an egg!" smiling emotionlessly once again.

I remembered vaguely that the priest had once quizzed me on this, and that he'd offered a rather lengthy theological explanation for it. As I searched my memory for the solution, the governor's voice roared from outside, "Checkmate!" He laughed. His laughter was as emotionless as the smile I'd seen on Chloe's face moments ago. "Check frigging mate!" he cried and rattled off a series of mutters that had the tone of a self-condemning lament. I could make out a phrase here and there along the lines of "What achievement..." "You're not even happy..." "I'm doomed..."

The soirée had dispersed; the governor was left alone in his drunken state, not unlike the other countless nights when he had come back from "work." Chloe left for her room, looking sad. I stopped her and whispered, "Hope you liked my surprise. Happy birthday!" She pecked me on my cheek—my first!—and she murmured, "Whose birthday party is this, anyway?"

I knew exactly how she felt—abandoned and used. I wanted to console her but couldn't find the right words; so I kissed her cheek and said nothing. To ensure maximum security over my investigation process, I said, "Remember, don't tell anybody what I told you."

She nodded abruptly and went off. I heard her door squeak and then it clicked.

*

CHLOE PLODDED OUT FROM her father's room the next morning, her head drooped, her face forlorn and dark. She passed me without looking at me. I caught her hand and asked, "Are you all right? Were you scolded? Is it because you disappeared from the party last night? Is it because he found out we were in my room all night? What is it?"

She said without looking at me, "I'm sorry, Lemonade. I'm so sorry, Iota," she repeated. She dashed into her room and slammed the door shut. I ran into mine and returned with my box of A–Z plant collection. I wrote a little note:

Don't be sad, princess. I will find X even if it means braving the ocean, I promise. Happy birthday, once more.—Lemonade

I placed the box by her door.

*

26

THE COTTAGE DOOR OPENED, and then it slammed right away in Barnett's face. It was past nine, in the early hours of the night, and he was half-drunk. He dropped heavily onto the steps of the cottage and studied with sunken eyes the little courtyard before him. He saw a fallen gutter dangling off the roof; the unattended shrubs of golden candle and Koster's curse wildly piercing one another's undefined territory; the once-immaculate lawn sprouting now with weeds; abandoned shovels and spades rotting right in the middle of it all; and the rusty hinges of the children's swing creaking in the wailing wind, its plank diseased with an un-scrubbed layer of thick moss. *Where are the hands that used to hold this forsaken house?* The man of the house was gone.

"I. Killed. You," Barnett trickled mournfully.

He turned to face the door that rejected him. "Yell at me, slap me, kick me, kill me for all I care, but please don't be quiet. Say something, please," he implored.

Barnett knew that it was not his fault, but he knew too that it was his responsibility. The man of the house had labored in sweat and blood for him since day one. He knew how much the worker loved his wife, and his wife, her husband. Barnett remembered how his worker, as a young father, leapt like a joyful child one day and cried of his firstborn, "He said 'Pa'! He called me 'Pa'!" Barnett buried his head into his quivering hands. Then he recalled the worker's smile, which was the same, sincere smile that he wore as much when he was reproached as when he was rewarded. Barnett now frowned in remorse at that smile. He relived his worker's endless yeses to him, rivaled only marginally by Ahiga's consider-it-done attitude. Then he revisited the night of the plantation fire in his mind—the panic, the anger, the confusion, the pain—and the ferocious flames that engulfed his loyal worker that was now burning within.

"I. Killed. You."

Barnett felt a fiery stab plunging deep into his heart. He clutched his chest. He clutched all his achievements from the day he turned his first million dollars over to his father to this very day when his house stood gloriously over Ahio, proclaiming his growing empire to the Pacific. He clutched everyone's applause, every word of esteem, every congratulatory handshake, every glass of celebratory champagne attributed to him through the years. He clutched them all in his trembling fist, his torn spirit devoid of pride and dignity, his expressive, exuberant, and self-exalting demeanor gone. He felt like the crushed remains of his canes dropping lifelessly from the grinder.

"What is the point of it all?" he wailed into the night.

The door behind him squeaked. The voice of a broken wife before her husband's murderer lamented, "Go away, you murderer of my children's hope, assassinator of my heart." She said it loudly, clearly, but not violently. She said it poignantly.

Chloe heard every word of it from the car. She wound the window up. Then she covered her ears and shook her head hysterically, and she shrieked wordless screams inside the car, none of which reached her father's deafened ears and deadened heart—deafened and deadened by inner screams of his own.

*

"HERMITS SHOW THE WORLD a fascinating fact about God," René directed his pupils to the cast of hermit crabs displayed in a glass tank. He scrawled three big words on the blackboard, underscoring the middle word:

GOD <u>IS</u> FATHER

"Stop thinking of God for a while as a person. Instead of thinking 'God is *a* Father,' try thinking, 'God *is* Father.' I know it sounds abstract, and it is at the beginning, but I assure you if you try, it will lead you to a most personal perception of God. I know it's difficult to grasp the idea, which is why I've brought my friends in to help me with this." He indicated the hermit crabs. "The scientific name for these hermits is *decapod crustaceans*. Like all crabs, the hermit has ten legs, thus 'decapod,' literally 'ten-footed'. Unlike other crabs, however, the hermit does not actually have a shell of its own." He teased his class, "Did you know that?

"The hermit has a very soft abdomen, making it easy prey even for the tiniest of fish. To protect itself from predators, the hermit salvages an empty shell left behind by a sea snail. Its long and spiraled abdomen then retracts and clasps firmly to the inner wall of the shell. The snail shell thus becomes a part of the hermit, which is why we call it a 'crab.' As the hermit outgrows the shell, it has to leave its old home for a bigger one.

"Here's the interesting part: when a bigger shell is available, a cast of hermit crabs will congregate around it, the bigger ones followed by the smaller ones. The biggest crab migrates to the newfound shell, following which the second biggest crab adopts the newly vacated shell, leaving its previous shell available for the next crab, and so on and so forth until all the hermits have migrated—from the largest to the smallest, completing what we call a 'vacancy chain.'" He paused to allow his class to marvel at the phenomenon. Then he continued, "That's the interesting part; now here's the fascinating part. If you connect the dots: the vulnerability of the hermit's abdomen, the salvaging quest, the salvaged shell, and the vacancy chain in which they all gather; a plan, an idea unfolds before your very eyes, yes?" He checked to see if the pupils were following, particularly those who were slower. Everyone nodded, except one.

"The hermits may have microscopic brains that enable them with visual and mechanosensory skills, which at best could only empower them with the intelligence to salvage. It is highly improbable they could pull off a plan of such macro complexity. Could they have planned something as complex as salvaging a protective device that comes from an entirely isolated line of causality? Could they have devised the idea of the vacancy chain?

"Improbable," the teacher answered his own question. Then he shut his eyes as if in deeper reflection, and said, "Impossible. They may have 'planned' to make the vacancy chain, but could they have planned the idea of the vacancy chain per se? Could they have invented the ecological system in which every hermit was provided for? Impossible." Then he inferred aloud, "Something or someone else did, and whatever it is that originally conceived the plan, it is necessarily intelligent; which means to say that there must be a mind behind it all." He chalked in bold, confident strokes on the blackboard:

PLAN = MIND = PROVIDENCE = FATHER = GOD

The school bell rang. The class applauded—more likely
for their dismissal than the "fascinating" demonstration from
their teacher—save one: Chloe. While every boy and girl
gushed out of the narrow gate of San Tommaso, Chloe
remained in her seat, her reddened eyes fixated on those first
three words on the blackboard.

*

RENÉ WAS ALL SET for his hammock siesta when Chloe
confessed everything she had heard at the cottage to him.
*Peace of mind must engage with, not detach from, the world's cry
for help—lest it become an escape*, he thought, to fortify
himself against the beckoning hammock. He unwittingly
recalled Barnett's subtle taunts over the years: "The saintly
life is fiesta, not siesta, Padre!" That knocked the temptation
of the hammock out of his mind with finality.

"Governor? I need your car," he spoke into the phone.

"Consider it done," Barnett's voice fuzzed on the other
end.

René hung up his phone and took Chloe with him. He
drove her round the island, pulling over every now and then.

He wound her through every place that was built by her father. He stopped at a newly erected bridge, and said, "See that bridge?" He stopped at the newer and bigger port: "See that big ship?" He stopped at a long strip of tarmacadam road: "See this? The first in the Pacific—no more bumpy rides in the future." He stopped by the side of the camouflaged barracks: "See? Hidden from Molan's watch now." He stopped by the bustling wet market: "See all these happy women shopping for their groceries?" He stopped before the new hospital annex and showed her the new beds and facilities: "See the recovering patients?" Then he detoured to Mount Ahio and arrived at the plantation, now five times its previous size.

"See what our governor, your father, has done for us all? It was a mistake, he didn't mean to kill the plantation worker," René said in his usual husky gentleness. "We all make mistakes, but we all do good, too. That's what being human is about. Your dad is human. So am I. So is everyone else. So are you. You've seen what he's done for Ahio, for us all—"

"But he's done nothing for me. He only uses me. He doesn't ask me if I'm happy. He only asks me about who has said what about him, or tells me to ask this or that person about this or that. He gets me to do things for him. He tells me to earn my keep and make myself useful. He says there's no free lunch in this world.

"But I'm his daughter," Chloe sobbed. "He's never home, and when he gets back late at night, I can't even tell him my problems, tell him about my stomachache, tell him about my schoolwork, tell him I got a big star on your assignment, tell him about my flowers, that they are blooming, tell him how much I love my little pillow, tell him I want him to carry me to bed and tell me a story. Because why? He's always too drunk for me.

"If God is Father, then God must be a user and a big liar who sets his own plantation on fire and kills his loyal worker," she lashed at René as if he were Barnett.

Both of them kept silent for a long time in Barnett's car, her soaked face on his warm, comforting paunch.

"Chloe?" René gently broke the convalescent silence.

She looked up sideward, one side of her face still resting on his belly.

"You're filled with hatred for your father. You're angry, which is why you're blinded to any good that comes from him. And that is hell you're living in. Can you do something for me, for yourself?"

She lifted her head slightly and nodded.

"I want you to notice."

"Notice?"

"Yes, notice. I want you to notice one good thing about your father a day and give me your report at the end of the year. You will have a list of two hundred and thirty-two good things about him by then.

"Sometimes, the darkness of one's hatred against another can be lit simply by noticing that one tiny light in a person."

"Sounds like fun! I'll try."

"Chloe?"

"Yes, Father?"

"Which comes first—the egg or the chicken?"

She giggled, sprang up, and chortled, "The egg in the chicken!"

*

27

THE PRIEST HAD WARNED ME about the warrior. The warrior had warned me about the governor. And the governor had warned me about the priest. All three had warned me about the skinhead. But no one had warned me about Chloe.

I sat alone by the sea on an ancient boulder. I loved it here. The massive rock had a slight dimple in its surface, as if it were made for the very purpose of sitting and silent contemplation: the ocean of one's emotions, the horizon of one's purpose, and the sky of one's spirit. The Pacific waves crashed onto the boulders beneath me, but the water could never break in—it was a natural seawall. Over here, I felt as if I could observe the thrills and spills of life without getting harmed. And it was here, I was told, that a mysterious explorer about one hundred years ago had docked his mighty schooner. I'd made this quiet corner of the island my private sanctuary.

"Chloe…Chloe…" the crashing waves seemed to call out to me.

"Why is she giving me the cold shoulder? What wrong have I done?" I replied.

"Nothing," the wind said.

"It's her, then?" I said.

The wind shook its head with the help of the swaying palms.

The ocean beckoned, "Look deeper in."

A crippled gull hopped a few wobbly steps before launching itself into the sky. *Maybe she's hurt?*

A gust of chilling wind divined, "What's cold in itself cannot give warmth."

I repeated the inner conversation aloud, "What's cold in itself cannot give warmth. Chloe, why are you so cold to me?"

Then came a voice from behind, a human voice: "You're troubled not by anything or anyone else but by your unmet need for warmth."

I jolted and turned around. "Pami? How did you know I was here?"

He smiled and said, "Thinking about Chloe?"

I nodded, and said, "She turned cold out of the blue. She doesn't even want me to chaperon her from school. When she comes back, she just shuts herself in her room. I've gone from knocking on her door to scaling the tree by her window, but she won't budge. It's disturbing how she's behaving."

"It's disturbing your needs are not met," Pami corrected. "How she is behaving has nothing to do with how you are feeling; how you are reacting has everything to do with how you are feeling," he explained. "That she's giving you the cold shoulder is one thing, that you're feeling troubled and disturbed by it is another.

"You are troubled because the fulfillment you get from her—be that attention, affection, appreciation—has suddenly ruptured."

I shut my eyes and dove deeply into Pami's wisdom. Pami kept silent.

I searched my feelings, verbalizing the process to my mentor, "I…I am…I am scared…I fear." I could hear the wind howling approvingly. "I fear that I might be abandoned. I'm also afraid that…that I may be hopeless, helpless, and useless." I opened my eyes gradually to meet the serenity of the setting sun before me, and Pami's quiet smile beside me.

"You are afraid that she might abandon you, like your father did, and like your mother did," Pami said. "Not that they did so intentionally.

"You are also afraid of being useless, like how you were so helpless when your father left you and when your mother drowned with the sinking ship."

"I see. So I am my problem?"

"It's not a problem. It's a situation. An unfortunate situation, it seems." Pami lifted his head toward the horizon and said, "But let's not judge too soon if this or that is in fact 'fortunate' or 'unfortunate.' There's still a long, long voyage ahead of us."

I followed his line of vision to meet the horizon. I nodded and said, "It's not over until it's over."

He smiled approvingly at me. "Iota Draconis! How apt—the star that glows distinctly in the cluster."

"Pami, what is it I need to do?"

"More like, what is it *we* need to do?" Pami sniggered in a mix of humor and lament. "Do our part, I guess."

"Which is?"

"We acknowledge our own needs for what they are—without judging ourselves. Then we take all our effort, but we also take our time—we do have a lifetime—to accept ourselves for all that we are. That way, we are giving to ourselves what we may otherwise need excessively from others: attention, appreciation, affection, and the permission to be ourselves, to be who we are. By and by, our love for ourselves will grow, which will naturally flow out as love for others. And as it does, we become more able to love and, correlatively, less expectant of others' love. One cannot love others if one does not love self."

"Wait!" I interjected when I saw Pami's lips parting for another doctrine. I shut my eyes to ingest what he'd said. "One cannot give what one does not already have," I voiced my thought. Pami looked at me with a slanted head, as if to say, "You're beyond your age."

Then he continued, "You can't expect to change Chloe's

behavior, but you can—gradually—change yourself."

"Can a person change?" I asked.

"The irony of all ironies—you can't change if you do not accept yourself. And when you do accept yourself for all that you are, you begin to change."

He looked at the horizon again. "Your goal lies out there, Iota. Be it your hope to change yourself, your hope to win Chloe's heart, or your search for your father. Do you know how to get there?"

I shook my head.

"Build the best boat, make the best oars, and strengthen your arms. Then paddle with all your might."

I cast my sight from the rocks to the sea, and into the horizon, and I shuddered at the distance. "I'm afraid I'll never get there, Pami."

"Your father, your Chloe, and your growth—your happiness. You cannot control happiness as if you'll get it when you will it. You may paddle with all your might and with all your heart, but listen—"

I listened.

"You do not move toward the horizon. It is the horizon that comes to you."

I understood what he said. I lifted my leg over my other knee and bounced my foot about. "Should I then sit around and wait?"

Pami laughed and shook his head. "Even the flowers need to act when the heavens pour. There's our part to play always. If you want to grow into a better person, you work at it with all your strength and let goodness come to you. If you want to win Chloe's heart, you work at it with all your might, and let her decide if she will come to you. If you want to find your father, you work at it with all your heart, and let the intricate details of the world bring him to you, if they do.

"We build the best oars, the best boat, and mighty arms—that's our part. And we paddle—that, too, is our part. As for the horizon, over which we have no control, it will decide on its own accord to meet us or not—that is not our part."

"Whose part is it, then?"

Pami shrugged his shoulders and afforded, "It's an intricate web of events and people. It's a mystery beyond me." He smiled profoundly.

Just about then, I saw a hermit crab walking sideward on the beach yonder. My sight followed its direction, and I saw hundreds of thin long lines in the sand scribbled by hundreds of hermit crabs. The hermit king must have found a bigger shell, I mused, as I recalled one of the lessons with Father René.

"Life provides," Pami breathed. "Life always provides. Do you want to be wealthy, like Chloe's father?" he asked.

It took me by surprise. "Hmm. I don't know, never thought about it. Maybe?"

"It's the same. You paddle with all your heart toward the horizon, but you don't move; it is the horizon that comes to you."

I supposed my face was showing doubt because Pami proceeded with a case in point that I'll never forget. He dashed to the hermits and returned with a little crab scrambling away between his fingers. He said, "What if I hid away all the shells in this world?"

I touched the little legs and said, "This fellow would never find a new home."

"No matter how hard it paddled," Pami concluded.

I frowned. "That's just so sad."

Pami smiled once again. "Nah, Love would never do that. It's just an example. But, even if I did hide away all the shells, it only means that I have something else in place for this fellow." He tickled the hermit's legs.

Point taken. Lesson learned. "But, so, what should I do?"

"Paddle."

"That's it?"

"And trust."

"And trust that my horizon will come to me?"

"Paddle hard, and trust that *the* horizon will come to you."

He handed me the hermit crab, stood up, and gazed into the vast distance. The evening sun above the horizon cast a shimmering path from the offing, to the sea, onto the crashing waves beneath us, finally glinting over my legs and my hands.

He said to me, "Iota, the horizon may be nearer than you think."

*

28

BARNETT PAID THE WIDOW a hefty solatium from his pocket and grieved through two sleepless nights. On the third day, he was up and around, reigniting his bout for boys against Ahiga. The trader needed boys for the laborious process of gathering, transporting, chopping, grinding, and planting sugarcane; the warrior to defend a vulnerable frontier weakened by the absence of a king.

It was an unusually windy afternoon and René had deduced that a powerful easterly had swept through the Pacific in the morning. The wind had sent a few sheets of paper tumbling into his school foyer. He picked one up, removed his spectacles, and squinted at the printed words:

TASTE THE SWEETNESS OF SUCCESS

Experience the alchemic science of sugar crystallization. Discover the secret art of optimal sugar processing. Begin your road to success. Today.

Meet Mr. Barnett Ahio in person and let him share with you his secret to success. Discover your career with the man who turned our island into a powerful economy of the Pacific. Come early to enjoy free sugar and candy giveaways!

René was tucking the pink flyer into his sleeve when a

few blue sheets whooshed across his face. He managed to nip one with his surprisingly nimble fingers. He turned it over and read:

BE A MAN—DEFEND YOUR LOVED ONES

Meet Commander Ahiga and witness his renowned "Flying Mantis" execution. Discover what it takes to be a real man; a man of integrity, honor, and fortitude.

René was flabbergasted. He stomped out of the building, plodding in the direction of the tumbling flyers.

Barnett and Ahiga had decided to raid San Tommaso that morning. They now stood apart, each with his army of recruiters armed with flyers—The Barnettans versus the Ahigans—pink on one side, blue on the other. René saw red. "Just what the hell do you think you're doing here?" The priest patted his chest repeatedly. Then his hands opened in resignation, "Will you please grow up?"

"Grow up? We won't even exist," Barnett hissed, "if no one chops those damned canes and sends them to the mill, let alone 'grow up.'"

"Nobody's contesting your importance, Barnett. And I do understand that boys are a pressing need on both ends,"— he shuttled his finger between Barnett and Ahiga—"but peace is imperative. I'm telling you for the umpteenth time—no society can exist without peace. And your ongoing fight for boys is eating into every inch of space on this otherwise peaceful island. I do not deny"—he peered into Barnett's eyes—"the need for a sound economy,"—and shifted to Ahiga—"nor the need for a formidable defense. Not a bit. But please. There's a time and place for everything, and your fight is not here, as far as I'm concerned. Here is where children learn to be civic. And your touting behaviors are hardly civic."

"Father," Ahiga implored, "if I didn't come, he would have taken every boy that's left." He glanced sideward at Barnett and snarled, "Let's see if the pirates or that tyrant will seize your sugar without a fortified defense." He turned back to René. "To raise boys of fortitude—we must." He flashed a glance at Barnett. "And boys of integrity."

"Yes, yes," Barnett crooned. "And let's see if the boys of 'might' and 'integrity' can hold the fort without money for their armory. Speaking of which, Commander, your firearms are on their way as we speak.

"You're most welcome!" he concluded his assault abruptly.

"Enough, please," said René, thrusting his palm in the air. He proceeded in a solemn tone, "Can we or can we not come to an agreement that your unruly squabbles and campaigning should be kept far and away from my school compound?"

"Only if he agrees," Ahiga offered.

René stared at Barnett, conveying his point without saying it.

"All right," Barnett relented. "Holy grounds, right?" He craned his neck toward René and whispered, "Don't forget to pick up your stash tonight!" He sniffed the air, as if savoring a good wine bouquet, and continued in the priest's ear, "Just arrived from Saint-Emilion. Grand Cru, Padre. *Chateau Ausone*, Padre. A rare '61 vintage, Padre," and, withdrawing his face from the pastor's reddened ear, he proclaimed, "Oh man of the *spirit*."

"A boy!" a navy warrior roared repeatedly, "A boy!" sprinting as he did toward the three men. "In the sea!" he gasped.

"After you!" Ahiga hollered and galloped after the messenger. Barnett ambled behind in quick steps like a pedigreed stallion, followed by René, trotting, clumsily negotiating his long fluttering cassock.

*

THE SKINHEAD TREADED IN THE SEA, gasping, spitting saltwater, and making one-way conversations to the motionless boy. The casualty was adrift and afloat on a pair of inflated pajamas. "How clever! Your mind has saved you, boy. Hang in there, hang in there!" Pahi`umi`umi breathed in deeply, and out, and in, and he dove under the float and exhaled into the boy's survival "raft."

He emerged, gasping, and he extricated the haversack from the boy's shoulder to lighten the weight. He was about to haul the casualty to his fishing boat when he heard a splash in the distance. He stopped and looked in that direction. He saw several more splashes, followed by warriors swimming in his direction. He breathed in, and out and in, and ducked under the water, reemerging some fifty yards away next to his boat. He submerged half his head and watched the rescue orchestrated by Ahiga. When the rescuers were gone, he mounted his boat swiftly and sped to the other side of the island, from where he sprinted to his cave with the boy's haversack across his shoulder.

*

"FIFTEEN," AHIGA ESTABLISHED.

"Seventeen," countered Barnett.

"Sixteen?" René offered.

The three men towered over the young casualty, throwing guesses at his age. Barnett picked up the deflated float—a pair of crumpled pajama pants knotted at the cuffs—and exclaimed, "What a smart fellow! Bright!" Lifting the soaked pajamas by his fingers, he turned to the other men.

"I want him!" he demanded, in a tone that was half-serious, half-joking, and fully covetous.

"If he pulls through," René rebutted. The exhausted priest flapped his arms to cool his body, overheated from all that trotting. He turned to Ahiga, who was wet and heaving, and said, "Is he going to make it?"

Ahiga knelt beside the boy and conducted his first-aid procedure, checking his eye dilation and pulse. "The boy is fine," he reported.

"Shipwreck, you reckon?" René asked.

"Looks like it," Ahiga replied.

"Any other things or persons found with him?" Barnett asked.

"Negative. He was alone. There was a boat more than fifty yards away from him, but it didn't look like it had anything to do with the boy. It's one of our fishing boats."

"Was there anyone in it?" Barnett pursued.

"Negative. Looks like it was anchored to the sand bar at low tide."

René looked at the boy and sighed. "It must be the easterly that wrecked this poor fellow. He should have drowned, or made a succulent feast for the sharks."

"It's a miracle, I must say," said Ahiga.

"Oh, now you're believing?" René teased.

Ahiga looked at the boy and shrugged. "How can I not?"

Barnett checked his gold pocket watch and said, "Commander, it's time."

All of a sudden, the boy burst into hysterical laughter. The three men jumped back. Then they laughed, nudging one another as frightened kids do. "All right, he's fine!" said Ahiga. "Maybe a tad…" Barnett drew imaginary circles at his temple.

"My bag!" the boy spouted and passed out.

"He's fine. He's all right, I'm sure," René said.

Ahiga took another look at the casualty.

"Go ahead, I'll stay with him," René offered.

Barnett and Ahiga, along with the navy warriors, headed off to a new shiny motorcar with the inscription "The Governor" on its side.

"Excited, Commander?" Barnett made conversation.

"It's been a long wait, Governor. How many prototypes have they delivered?"

"Let's see. Seven pistols, two rifles, two semi-autos, five naval guns, couple of sea mines…."

*

29

FOR NO PARTICULAR RHYME or reason, Chloe became warm again. It felt like my horizon had drifted to me; and the funny thing was, I hadn't particularly paddled my boat. Perhaps, as Pami had taught, an intricate collusion of events had taken place unbeknownst to me, and like an invisible hand, it had brought my "horizon" back to me. This was some mystical concept I hadn't completely fathomed; all the same, I relished Chloe's "return" to me with eternal gratitude. I was back at San Tommaso to resume my chaperoning.

The phone rang while I waited for my princess at the Father's office. Father René picked up the phone, and started speaking. "San Tommaso—" "Governor?" He glanced at me. "Yes, he's with me." "Tree house?" "Now?" "Are you speaking in sobriety?" "Okay." Then he turned to me and said, "The governor wants you at the tree house."

I had no idea why I was being summoned to the tree house, the "Official Meeting Place of the Fathers." *Obey and trust, says the commander.* So I nodded.

"Father, what is *sobriety*?" I enquired, in part to size up the weight of the situation, and in part to learn a new word.

"Eavesdropping, huh?"

Eavesdropping? You're hardly a yard from me! "Yes, sorry," I said. *How come adults are always right?*

"*Sobriety* is the state in which one is sober, clear minded...and free from alcohol's influence," the Father taught. He appeared to be thinking about something after he voiced the last remark. "How often does he come home drunk?" he probed.

"He?" said I, not knowing to whom he was referring.

"Sorry—I meant your guardian, the governor."

I was mentally counting the nights he had come home babbling ugly things about himself, about life, in a drunken stupor, when I decided to count the nights he returned in sobriety instead.

"None."

"None?"

"Sorry—I meant none in sobriety," I said, taking pride in using the new word.

He nodded, still appearing deep in thought; and he murmured, "He wants you right away." It was as if his mouth was detached from his mind.

*

THE GOVERNOR'S SHINY MOTORCAR was already waiting outside for us. *That fast?* I thought. It felt like that "intricate

214

collusion of events unbeknownst to me" except that this was obviously planned by another person, by the governor. It was some distance to the tree house, so I decided to make good use of it. I proceeded with my investigation of the prime suspect.

"Father, have you heard of San Tommasi?"

It seemed that the mention of the place swung his mind back from outer space. He looked at me with widened eyes. I thought I had him nailed until he opened his mouth, "How do you know of this place? Why, yes. It's one of the cities in Dartnorth," he ruffled my head, and said, "You're growing in wisdom and knowledge. I'm impressed!"

That certainly did not sound like he had any association with San Tommasi, the place where I was born and raised. The Father, it seemed, was not, after all, my father. *Wait,* a voice in my head commanded, *it could be a decoy!* I dodged his compliments and persisted in my interrogation. "Are San Tommasi and San Tommaso the same?"

"Yes, they refer to the same person: St. Thomas of Aquinas."

Ha! I'm getting close. "Have you been to San Tommasi?"

"Yes," he said.

Checkmate! I thought.

"And no," he added.

No!

"I was there for a couple of hours, waiting to board my vessel at the harbor, and that was it. Beautiful place, it is. I wish I'd toured around. So, would you regard that as a 'yes' or a 'no'?"

My mind being rid of all hope, I was no longer in the mood to continue my conversation with him. I kept quiet the rest of the ride, which was a lot less bumpy than before due to the newly planed road, which reminded me of the man who built it—the governor. *Could Mr. Barnett be the man who'd abandoned my mother and me? Is he my father? Is that why he summoned me to the tree house?*

*

NO SOONER HAD I ENTERED the tree house than the commander shot a question at me like the semi-auto weapon he had recently acquired: "You said the skinhead was onboard the royal vessel the day it sank?"

"I said?" I said.

"You said," he said. "Who said?" he then said.

"Chloe said," the governor said.

"Chloe said?" I said.

"You said," he said.

"Who said?" the commander said.

"He said," the governor said.

"I said?" I said.

"Who said what?" Father René said, ceasing our rattling exchange of gunfire.

"All right, I said," I said. *I'll have it out with you, Chloe Ahio!*

The governor inched toward me, sniffing his purple handkerchief repeatedly, and hissed, "I smell a rat."

My commander fired off another round at me. "Tell us, what have you heard? Who have you been talking to? What have you been doing behind our backs?"

I instinctively took cover behind the Father's white robe. He said, "Hush, gentlemen. It's unbecoming to treat a juvenile in this manner even if he's been convicted of a crime. Fear will only breed more fear, and the more fear, the more rage, and the more rage, the more acts of crime." He gently shoved me out from behind his frock. "Come, tell us what happened. What have you said, child? What have you done?"

There was a calming effect to the priest's husky voice, such that I felt less coerced into confession. I told them everything, including Pami's secret that he was on the royal vessel when it sank, and that according to Pami's eyewitness account, the only one we had, the king's ship was wrecked by a natural disaster, and not, as many—including the governor—alleged, by Queen Molan. To my surprise, the three old men looked anything but punishing. Apart from the governor—who looked quietly nervous biting his fingernails—the other two men seemed overwhelmed by a strange mix of shock, wonder, confusion, relief, and gratefulness. I'd never thought I possessed such capacity to silence three big men, the Fathers of Ahio at that. It took them a while before someone could speak.

"So!" the warrior suddenly thundered, his murderous eyes upon the governor. "The majesty's shipwreck had nothing to do with Molan! You made it all up—just to raze your old plantation for one that's five times the size! You knew that the only acceptable reason to burn your plantation was to protect innocent lives from Molan. You—" The warrior was seething. He aimed his mouth at the governor, and blasted, "You son of a bitch!"

The priest covered my ears immediately, muffling the warrior's curses: "What fire of self-sacrifice, which you so heroically lit 'for the safety of our people'! What gun threat by Molan! What dire need to step up our armory! They're all your doing! A pack of lies, you are! You sneaky bastard, I'm going to kill you!"

Everything suddenly sounded incredibly loud when the Father released his hands from my toasty ears. He took the warrior aside, and whispered with incredibly amplified clarity, "Stay calm, stay calm. Breathe. Focus. Notice the women's laughter in the market, the recovering patients smiling with hope in the hospital, the ploughmen singing songs of harvest in the field, your fortified armory glimmering in the barracks. They are all just as real as his lies."

The governor, who always had an answer to everything, said nothing save these three words, "Guilty as charged."

That seemed to simmer the warrior's anger.

"Now, who exactly is the skinhead to be on the king's vessel?" Father René diverted the commander's furious attention from the governor. "Could he be the captain or the crew?"

"No. I personally detailed the men," the warrior said.

"The cook?"

"Him, too."

"One of the butlers?"

"Those, too; I cleared them personally. We had to ensure maximum security."

Father René scratched his head and muttered, "Why then was the skinhead on the king's vessel, if not—"

"If not that he's of royal blood," the governor inferred aloud.

"King Ahio's brother?!" The priest looked incredibly surprised.

"The skinhead is a prince of Ahio!" The warrior's eyes glimmered with resurrected hope. He looked at me, beseeching an affirmation, "Has he told you that?"

I shook my head.

"He's got to be Prince Ahio," he insisted. "The dynasty lives!" the warrior exclaimed repeatedly, shaking his head in disbelief.

"But why must he hide from everyone?" I asked.

The three old men shrugged.

"We'll find out soon," said the governor.

"To the vampires' den!" the warrior commanded.

*

I LED THE FATHERS of Ahio through all 2,241 paces into the innermost chamber of the prince's domain. It was my glorious moment, for it tremendously validated my competence. It was my unofficial induction into the brotherhood of men. I brought them to the green lake, shimmering in the middle, in the solitary beam of sunlight.

"The prince's hermitage!" the priest marveled with clasped hands.

"More like an infirmary, a lair, an asylum," the governor corrected.

"Palace," the warrior decreed.

"Palatial, indeed!" the governor agreed and disagreed in one breath. "Little wonder he'd long left that little tree house."

While the three men toured Pami's cave, I ran into his

bedroom to alert him of their intrusion, but he wasn't there. I dashed to the rabbits' nursing room, to the kitchen, and then into "Michelangelo's Chapel"—he was nowhere to be found. Pami had transformed the "chapel" ceiling into a colorful canvas of Ahio's proud history: the escape, the exile, the establishment, the countless battles against piracy, the prosperity and achievements. There was a note on the solitary stool. It was for me.

I came out of Michelangelo's Chapel, feeling sad after reading Pami's note. I said, "He's gone."

The governor snatched the note from my hand, and read it aloud:

I have gone through every record in the port annals. With the exception of Father René and Governor Barnett, no one on the island has set foot on San Tommasi. If it isn't either of the two, you may try looking for your father next on Isle of Molan when you get the chance. I must warn you, though, that the passage is treacherous. But I'm sure Commander Ahiga can help; he knows the safest route.

I must go. May the horizon find you prepared.

Godspeed, Iota Draconis.

Pami

P.S. Please ask Commander Ahiga to increase security in the barracks. I broke in without a sweat.

*

30

BARNETT, AHIGA, AND RENÉ took turns fathering the boy whom they believed had lost his vessel, his mother, and his memory to a shipwreck. The trader had liked him at first sight and wanted him for his brightness; the warrior was adamant to shield him from Barnett's use and wanted the boy as much for the boy's as his own security; the priest simply couldn't say no to a pathetic situation. The lost boy was provided for through and through—food, shelter, clothes, knowledge, and love—even as providence came through self-profiting motivations and the clumsy hands of the three men. At face value, it might seem that the boy was on the receiving end of kindness from the men, which was true, doubtless. But it was just as true that Iota Draconis was a bright, quiet boy who had given the old men, each in different and unexpected ways, a new surge of life.

Two weeks after René took the boy in to San Tommaso, the priest, feeling the heat from intensive fathering, escaped without a word to a remote islet. The celibate, not until now accustomed to the restlessness that came with every intimate relationship, tried to shake the boy off his mind through every available means. Alone on the islet, he slugged bottles of wine, stuffed himself with meats, and took several long naps a day in his hammock. Still, he kept thinking of the boy, who was left alone in the dormitory. *Does he know where I've kept the meats? Will he get himself burned by the stove? Does he know his way around? Will he get lost in the woods? Does he know where the clean pajamas are? Can he deal with the quiet nights alone?* On his third day in isolation, René suddenly realized that such "worldly" concerns were stemmed from the core of one's human makeup. Contrary to what he'd hitherto believed to be distractions from the divine, those burdens were in fact born of the divine—his restlessness of heart was something of Love. And anything that connects one with Love connects one with the divine. Thus he ended the retreat on the remote islet, resolved to engage the world and its needs more actively and positively. The priest was prepared to father Iota Draconis even if it meant a lifetime.

Through the boy, the warrior had learned that he did not need to always relate to people with rigidity. Iota Draconis had brought the laughter and softness out of Ahiga. And through the boy, specifically his ingenuous love for Chloe, Barnett would come to see the light that would eventually free him from his pensive drunkenness....

*

I DASHED OUT OF MY ROOM to make sure Chloe was not frightened, but realized immediately that she had camped over at San Tommaso. It was late in the night, and someone was pounding mightily on the governor's door. From the stair landing, I saw the back of my governor face-to-reddened-face with the man who pounded the door, which was now open. It was my commander.

I couldn't hear their exchange of words clearly from where I was, and just when I descended the stairs to investigate the commotion, the two men broke out into a scuffle. With a few swift maneuvers—which I, too, had learned from my commander—the governor's arms had been immobilized behind his head. His legs were kicking the door, the chairs, the coffee table, and everything else but his opponent, who was safely located and locked to his back.

"You! Get his legs!" my commander yelled at a butler, then at a male servant, then at a maid; but no one dared to budge.

I thought the scene was a tad ridiculous—the warrior ordering the governor's servants to apprehend their master.

"Young warrior! Where the hell are you?" my commander bawled.

Young warrior? Who? I wanted to feign ignorance.

"Iota Draconis!"

"Yes, sir!" I shot back. There being no other way out, I

"obeyed and trusted" my commander's...*command.* I dashed to the living room.

As soon as my commander caught sight of me, he ordered, "Evacuation procedure for drowning casualty!"

Drowning? Who? Where's the sea? I tried to think through the confusion swimming in my head.

Seeing my confusion, the warrior spelled out more specifically, "Procedure One: Immobilize struggling casualty!"

Are you kidding me?

"Warrior!" my commander thundered.

"Yes, sir!" I pealed.

"Now!" he exploded.

"No!" the governor imploded.

I closed my eyes and called to mind every bad image of the governor. I saw him using Chloe to get information about me, to betray me. I saw him night after endless drunken night neglecting Chloe, *my* Chloe. I clenched my fist and swung an uppercut into his imploring jaw. The "casualty" was successfully immobilized.

"Grab his legs!" was my next instruction, followed by, "Mount vehicle!" The next thing I knew, I was on my way to the prison cell with my commander on one side, and a captive who was fathering me on the other.

*

AHIGA ORDERED IOTA DRACONIS to drop the governor-turned-casualty-turned-convict and to wait outside the prison, with specific instructions not to enter. Then he slammed the door shut with his back and dragged Barnett to the prisoner-of-war chamber, where a water tank stared menacingly into the convict's eyes. "No!" the governor warned ineffectively.

Ahiga dunked his captive's head into the water until he almost drowned, repeating the treatment several times, each time yelling as his captive reemerged: "Are you not awake?" Then he cast his criminal aside and stood over him.

The exhausted captive slumped against the side of the tank and retaliated weakly, "How dare you. I'm the governor. What's all this about?"

"This isn't about our fight over boys," the warrior retorted. "This isn't about your pack of lies," he said.

"This is about your daughter," a familiar husky voice came from the corner.

"Accomplice…" the governor fizzled fecklessly.

"Are you not awake?" René repeated the warrior's question albeit in a much gentler tone. "Are you not done blanketing your guilt under your drunken stupor? Are you not done neglecting…using…hurting your own daughter?" His gentle tone simmered Ahiga, who now admonished the drunkard in like manner, "Burning your own plantation and co-worker, and all the countless lies you sold to your faithful workers, your partners, your only daughter, and yourself. And after all that's been done, you drown your guilt in your golden brew and run the risk of losing everyone? For what, Barnett? For a plantation five times the size? For a big fat bank account? For a new sugar mill, which you conveniently turned into your private residence? For what? Personal achievement? Are you not awake? Are you not aware or do you pretend not to be aware that your so-called personal achievements are not yours alone? That all that you possess is the result of many people's work, sweat, and blood? That without the wind that carried the rain to your harvest, your plantation—five times, ten times, one hundred times bigger, no matter—is nothing but parched scraps of earth? That without the gratuitous richness of our soil your acres of plantation are nothing but barren mud?

"Awake, brother! Before you lose everything and everyone. We can only do this once for you; thereafter, it's all up to you."

Barnett was so grieved to hear the truth—that which he had avoided with all his power—he would have dunked himself into the tank without help had he not felt the genuine care of the two men.

René knelt beside the slumped governor on one knee and said, "Acknowledge your contribution, your success. By all means drink and celebrate your accomplishments, which we, together with every man and woman and child of Ahio, profoundly appreciate. But claim only what is truly yours."

Ahiga continued, "It's your choice: your love for exaggerated—delusional—glory, or the true love of your daughter?"

He whipped out a copy of the governor's speech that René had drafted to combat the mass rally, and through which Barnett was made to publicly resolve to "take up his scepter" to defend what he loves, and "to cooperate" for Ahio's future "with all his heart and soul." And he slipped the resolution into Barnett's hand. As the two men departed from the crushed aristocrat, René turned his respectful eyes to him and said, "Barnett, I admire you not for what you've done or accomplished but for who you are—your inner drive, your ability to motivate people to be the best they can be, and your rare capacity to arouse one from siesta to fiesta—by virtue of who you are. Value is not always measured by how much a person has or has done—have you not seen with your own eyes the boy's ingenuous love for your daughter? Chloe hasn't done a thing; yet Iota treasures her for who she is, not for what she's done. There are things we can learn from a child, Barnett.

"And like a child's heart, there's beauty in every man's soul only to be reclaimed and relived. We'd lost our innocence to betrayals and subsequently the fear of betrayals.

But why should we ever lose that which makes us truly valuable to the world—"

"Oh grow up, kiddo!" Barnett scoffed in a sudden outburst of vitality. "What are you—Peter Pan in a religious cloak?" He sniggered. "The coming of age is the weaning from one's innocence, no?

"Be realistic!" he barked.

"Be real!" René rebutted. "Stop fluffing your need for innocent love just because no one in the 'realistic' world plans to fulfill it—or should I say—is able to fulfill it. You need love, don't you, old boy? Which is precisely why you're dressing up—your suits, your fleet of motorcars, your hilltop palace, and what have you—for it. For love!"

Barnett slumped back against the water tank.

"Please don't lose the beauty of your soul, old boy."

"But my soul is stained," Barnett confessed and collapsed into sobs.

"Yes, it is, I'm afraid. But aren't we all stained? Pardon my unorthodoxy—it is precisely our stains that make us truly valuable. Of what value is Love if it is only given to those who aren't stained? No, the fact is we all are stained, and we all are blessed in abundance, *still*. The sun shines for everyone, and the rain pours on everyone, stained or unstained."

"Ha!" Barnett cried cynically. He looked at his soaked state and rolled his eyes at Ahiga, and he muttered, "Showers of blessing—indeed. This much I agree: that we all are stained." His eyes glanced away sharply from the man who'd manhandled him. "Disdainful," he scorned quietly.

Ahiga gazed at Barnett's sorry state, and then at the water apparatus. "Guilty as charged," he convicted himself.

René felt at that instant a sudden urge to run for the nearest hammock. He steadied himself and made for the prison door. He turned around and said to Barnett, "By the way, you did shake me up from my siestas, simply by walking your talk, 'Fiesta, *not* siesta.'" He took one more look at the dark ceiling of the cell, the mottled walls, and the water tank, and he said, "Don't stay here too long, old boy."

*

31

IT DIDN'T MAKE SENSE TO ME—the governor who provided for me making use of his own daughter; the priest who pastored me, abandoning his flock from time to time; and the warrior who disciplined me manhandling the governor. I didn't need to know what happened after my commander shut me outside the prison cell, and I didn't want to know; but the way he used me to seize the governor already didn't seem right. Yet, I could not deny that my guardian had spent a lot more time with Chloe since that night. Everything about this island felt strange all over again.

I made for my secret place where Pami had appeared the last time. I was hoping he would appear again, that another of my many horizons would come to me. But it never did. I tried talking to nature again to see if that might invoke his presence, but that didn't work, either. I was very much taken with him despite the many things I didn't know about him. Now that he'd gone, I felt like I had so much to ask him— like why's he always hiding from the three old men, from the world; and why he wore an eye tattoo at the back of his neck. *Someday, maybe?* I thought. *If I ever see you again.*

I sat quietly on my favorite boulder. What if I could

never find my pa? And what if Pami were gone forever? I wondered in my troubled heart, *What will become of me?* Thinking about my uncertain future with these strange men in this strange place, I shuddered in a gust of chilly wind, and wrapped myself under my arms.

I looked at the evening's calico sky—blue, purple, orange, and yellow—seeping into the horizon, and the sea from the horizon spewing its reflection into a reversed order of yellow, orange, purple, and blue. "Beauty." I breathed the word Pami had used to describe my mother. I used it to describe the sunset before my eyes. It was beautiful, the colorful sky, and equally beautiful the sea that mimicked the sky. An aching hope rose from my heart to part my lips, "Mom, pa, are you out there?" I asked the horizon.

Mother Nature said nothing. Or it could be that my mind did not have an answer. I thought of the great whites that were migrating, preying, mating, or simply wandering in the dark under the beautiful ocean, feeling around and sensing about without a good pair of eyes. *Sometimes you need to shut your eyes—in order to see.* Pami's words shone like a pin of light in the darkness of my unknowing, just a glimmer, just a glimpse, just like the flickering star after which I'd been named—Iota Draconis. I closed my eyes to see.

I saw myself.

I saw a boy, shipwrecked, lying helplessly in a strange

place. I saw a frightened boy, frightened by his own anxious thoughts, frightened by…nothing. I saw a boy in need, and I saw a strange man coming to his aid. He'd walked with me, cooked for me, clothed me, sheltered me, and given me his knowledge, his wisdom, his warmth, his peace—he'd given me a part of himself. I saw a boy in need of guidance, and I saw another strange man coming his way—he, like the first man, had clothed and sheltered me, but unlike him, disciplined me, admonished me, and guided me, and given me swords, skills, and strength. He'd given me security—a part of himself. Then I saw a boy in need of the colors of life, vivacity, and freedom, and I saw yet another stranger, a colorful one, crossing his path. He'd given me clothes and shelter, and space to explore things and people. He'd shared a part of himself, which I'd perceived as the mental dexterity necessary to deal with life's challenges, to transcend life's adversities, to rise, to progress, to excel, to grow. I saw a boy in need of significance and nurturance, and a stranger the world denounced as "demonic" met his eyes in that one moment of chance collusion. He'd nurtured me with a deep understanding of myself, and affirmed me of my innate significance.

I saw too, a boy who had grown a lot in a short time. And along with growth, I saw my need, my turn to share a part of myself. It was then that the world's most beautiful girl, by my standard at least, stood before me, extending her friendship to me. Then from nowhere I felt my manhood fall upon my grateful lap at the very proud moment when I led the Fathers of Ahio into the prince's cave. I had been provided for, more than I could ever imagine. I marveled at what I saw.

I wondered if I'd ever marry Chloe. She was why I'd decided to stay at the Barnett residence. To be sure, I was furious to find out that she'd told my secret to her father. But I thought about the morning when she walked out of her father's room. I recalled the remorse with which she'd apologized to me. And my anger dissipated instantly. *Have I not betrayed Pami's secret too? Who am I to judge?*

Everyone wants a good ending, and so did I. I wondered if the Fathers concurred with Pami's wisdom—that the horizon of the trader's success, the horizon of the warrior's safety and security, and the horizon of the Father's serenity had "legs" of their own. I wondered if I'd ever see Pami again. I wondered if I'd return to San Tommasi where I'd come from or if I'd stay on Ahio for the rest of my life.

I wondered if I'd ever find pa.

I know. I could do something about my quest even as I wondered uncertainly. I could find the best timber with the help of Father René, and emulate his calm disposition. I could build the sturdiest oars and the safest boat, through discipline and tenacity from Father Ahiga. And I could steer my boat through the treacherous Pacific with Father Barnett's steady hands and shrewdness. Above all, I could hope.

I saw in the darkness of my mind the glimmer of light that flooded blindingly into every corner. I opened my eyes and relished the colorful sky above, and the sea mimicking the sky below, and I spouted the words Pami had given me, that little spark that set my mind aglow: "Sometimes you need to shut your eyes—in order to see."

I saw something else. That even as I was bereft of my mother, even as I may not have found pa and that I may never find him, even as I may have lost Pami forever—there was still the comforting and reassuring presence of the Fathers of Ahio. Through them, I saw something of Love, something of Light, something of a providential plan that belonged to none of us. It was a perfect plan. If then there was a plan, surely there must be a mind, and if the mind belonged to none of the Fathers, to whom does it belong? I pulled out a new notebook from my haversack and I jotted on the first page:

MIND = PLAN = PROVIDENCE = FATHER = LOVE

Iota, the horizon may be nearer than you think. Pami's words flashed before me. *Maybe the quest is the purpose? Maybe the journey is the destination? Maybe I'm already sailing on the horizon?* I may not have found pa, but I'd certainly seen and received Love. *Maybe—like me—the Fathers of Ahio are also seeking their "pa"? Doesn't the warrior seek security? Doesn't the trader continually seek the higher place in life? Doesn't the priest seek refuge from a dangerous world?* I turned a new page and wrote:

EVERYONE IN THIS WORLD, EACH IN DIFFERENT WAYS,
SEEKS THE SAME FATHER.

I thought of my first dinner on Ahio Island, where the priest had provided for me: sizzling steak, pajamas, a warm bed, and a familiar song. My lips flowered into a jubilant whistle, and the chirpy notes of "Hilary's Song" filled the calico twilight. And its lyrics filled my calico mind.

It all made sense.

*

THE GOVERNOR SNAPPED HIS FINGERS at one of his butlers. He was in his brown suit and white shirt, starched all over, his purple handkerchief flirting at me from across the dining table. His outstanding green eyes were glowing with the same exuberance I'd seen through my salt-infected eyes. It was the same man with the same peacock crown I'd seen the day I'd drifted onto the Island of Ahio. Chloe was by his side.

"Two pegs of whiskey," he instructed his butler, clinking the crystal glass with his silver spoon. He considered for a moment and added with much pride, "And a half."

He turned his head around the table. "Gentlemen?"

"Equal measure in Bordeaux, please," Father René replied.

"Same, please," the warrior intimated five fingers at the host.

Everyone at the table looked at me, much to my surprise. *Me? A gentleman, too?*

"Lemonade, *pwease,*" Chloe purred and giggled.

Everyone laughed.

I was saved from embarrassment by the butlers and maids. Glasses were filled as requested, and the maids presented our appetizers on silver-domed platters, much to every diner's delight—mine especially. They removed the lids to reveal piled periwinkles steaming with ginger and white wine. My stomach growled as soon as the aroma reached my nose.

"Grace, gentleman?" Father pointed me out.

Chloe giggled once more.

I rattled off, "Thank you, God. Thank you, Provider of sun and soil, and rain and wind, so that we have food for our body. Thank you, Provider of fathers and mothers, sons and daughters, friends and families, lovers, and brothers and sisters, so that we have food for our spirit. Thank you, Provider. Thank you, Father!"

I was pleasantly surprised that I'd completed my prayer without a hitch, as was Father René, who watched me with one eye throughout my eloquent delivery. At the end of my prayer, he winked at me approvingly.

"Let me propose a toast!" the governor offered. "Let me see, what shall we drink to?" He shut his eyes to think, and he said, "Here's to prosperity!"

"Is that all you care about, *Governor?*" the warrior teased.

My guardian shrugged. "What to do. I'm first a trader— and always so—then a politician." His eyes darted back and forth, as if thinking. "How about this?" He raised his lowball glass again. "Here's to progress! *Our* progress!" he added, his head inclined toward his daughter.

"And here's to peace!" the Father added.

"And to Prince Ahio!" the warrior said. "And to the great kings since Ahio I, without whose light and sacrifice we would have none of this." He spread his hands over the scrumptious fare.

"In that case, we must also drink to Twiitaga!" the governor said, "without whom there would not have been Ahio I."

Twiitaga? Who is Twiitaga? Why does that name ring a bell? Do I know Twiitaga? I spewed my thoughts: "Who is

238

Twiitaga?"

Father René chuckled and said, "That's a dangerous question to ask. Why, because everyone gives you a different answer. Best to hear it from the horse's mouth."

Then I suddenly recalled what Pami once muttered to himself, which I found unpalatable then (not that I understood now): *Where there's light, there too is Twiitaga.* I asked the priest, "Where can I find the answer?"

"The Treatise on Twiitaga," he replied.

The governor looked skeptical. "Is there such a thing?"

The warrior nodded.

Father René said to my guardian, "I always wondered why you built such a mammoth library in your house—"

I interjected excitedly, "Yes! He has over twenty thousand books! And they all look and feel new!" I realized immediately I might have appeared malicious.

The men laughed.

The priest continued, "Now I know. Why—the Treatise is in your library, old boy!"

We laughed. I could not recall the last time I'd laughed so heartily.

Chloe rose abruptly and made for the music player, while the servers prepared the table for our second course. "I want to dance," she said as "Hilary's Song" flowed from the big horn, sending all the men into merriment. Even the warrior's rigid fingers were drumming to the melody. Chloe and I danced. My heart was half with her and half with the fathers whose conversation was within earshot.

"So was it true that Molan gave you a pistol as a threat in disguise?" the warrior asked the governor.

"That Molan gave me a pistol is a fact. That she'd meant it as a threat is my conjecture, a measured one," the governor crooned. "Do you seriously think that she would give me something out of good will?"

"Why not?" the priest interjected. "There's no one in this world so evil there isn't any good in her. Conversely, there isn't anyone so good there's no evil in her."

"Says who?" the governor retorted.

"Says Twiitaga," the warrior answered.

The governor shrugged indifferently, and sighed, "That queen is just as capricious as the Pacific." He lifted his whiskey glass to his lips.

"Hilary's Song" ended. Chloe and I returned to the table, and dinner resumed. What with the girl I loved and my revered Fathers of Ahio sharing the table, it would take more courage to make a declaration than to execute an uppercut to the governor's jaw. I decided nonetheless to be a brave warrior and a fine gentleman midway into dinner.

"Lady"—I dipped my head in Chloe's direction—"and gentlemen…" said I, with as much manliness as I could possibly infuse into the tone. Every mouth stopped chewing. Every pair of eyes turned to meet mine.

"To find my pa—I must. I shall therefore rise to meet the unpredictability of the Pacific and the queen." I withdrew my flashlight from my pocket. "Fret not," I said, uncertain if I were reassuring my audience or myself, "for this little light will pave my way step by each unknown step—small and big—into the future.

"I shall make my voyage to the Isle of Molan."

While everyone looked impressed with my courageous announcement, the governor rose from his seat and hovered behind me. He squeezed my shoulders and whispered suggestively, "Why the Isle of Molan? Could I not be your father?"

I said, "Apart from Father René, whom I've learned had made the vow of chastity"—I had no idea why the governor sniggered—"you are the only one in Ahio who's been to San Tommasi and back. But you are not my father. Why, because firstly, you would have hastened to acknowledge your identity, which you didn't—"

"And why would I do that?" the governor sought.

"Our relationship would give you ample reason to have me in your business."

It was the priest's turn to snigger. As did the rest.

"And secondly, were you my father, you would have

stopped me from courting your daughter, which you didn't."

"Brrr—ight!" the governor exclaimed. As did the rest. They raised their glasses at the governor's cue, "Here's to the star from the north, Iota Draconis!"

Having received such enormous confidence from the Fathers of Ahio, I winked at Chloe, who—for the first time since I met this most beautiful girl in the world—blushed and looked away.

* * *

EPILOGUE

· · · · · · · · · · ·

THE FUTURE KING OF AHIO fell into a deep sleep, after consuming two whole spring chickens and some wine. "Thank you, thank you…" he muttered in his sleep, eternally grateful for the explorer's kindness.

Twiitaga smiled. He got to his feet, gathered the chicken foil, recorked the unfinished bottle of wine, and dropped everything into his huge duffel bag. He sat by the future king and relished the night. Above him, the stormy clouds had given way to millions of stars. They reminded him of humankind. *How easy for one man to forget his own significance in the expanse of this world.* He cast a gentle glance at the future king, who fidgeted in his slumber.

Twiitaga whispered.

"Do you wonder how you've ended up in this

situation—this forsaken place with this clueless multitude? Your troubled heart may tell you that all of this is a mistake.

"It is not. Where you are right now is not a mistake, even though it feels like one. Where you are right now is the result of an epic collusion between you and the Universe.

"Did you have any foreknowledge of the whirlwind that swept you ashore?

"Did you have any foreknowledge of this island?

"Did you time everything such that every thing and person and event coincided with your intent?

"No.

"And that's the good news.

"Why? Because you now know that Life is not out to harm, but help, you.

"So why do you doubt yourself when the Universe entrusts its future to you?

"That you're troubled by your tribe can only mean that you have them in your heart."

The future king fidgeted once more.

"I understand why you withdrew from the flock, and I think it is necessary for one to be in solitude from time to time. Yet peace of mind must engage with, not detach from, the world's cry for help—so that solitude is not an escape from reality.

"Well, by all means, do escape from time to time. But

come back always."

Twiitaga laughed melancholically and said, "There's nothing in reality that one needs to escape from."

He felt his stubbled chin and said, "Be not overly anxious about the unknown future. Have some faith that Good will always prevail—whatever reality may suggest, and however ominous you may feel.

"Be humble—we must," he continued. "But always remember that Life does not intend to suppress humankind, because everything in this world is destined to excel, to soar to greater heights—the world cannot but progress.

"Face your adversities, no matter their magnitude, as if they are opportunities to reach greater heights—indeed to arrive at human greatness.

"Set your eyes on the horizon, but keep your mind open always. Put your hands on the oars and put all your heart into the paddling—the horizon will come to you.

"But first, ascertain with what little light you have if the horizon is worth pursuing—as you have done for yourself tonight."

Twiitaga dug into his bag and emerged with the bottle of wine. He uncorked it and took two sips.

"Sleep well, future king. I must go. I'm an explorer."

Twiitaga rose to his feet, shouldered his duffel bag, and walked toward the monstrous silhouette of the three-sail schooner. He put the flashlight in a wooden box, placed it on a huge boulder along the natural seawall, and climbed onto the schooner. He turned around and said to Prince, the future king, "An explorer is everywhere—if you should wish to find me."

*

"WHO IS TWIITAGA?"

The bright clear sky revealed the clueless expressions of the exiles.

Prince persisted, "Did you not see an explorer last night?"

No one had seen him.

"Surely you must have seen his schooner?" Prince spread his arms to illustrate a huge vessel.

No one had seen it, either.

"The schooner!" Prince exclaimed and dashed along the footprints he had left the night before. He arrived at the site where he had met the explorer. He surveyed the long line of naturally stacked boulders extending from the coastal rocks into the sea, at the tip of which the schooner was previously docked—it was gone.

"The flashlight!" he remembered. He searched all his pockets but found nothing.

One of the men came running with a wooden box.

"Prince! I found this over there," he reported, pointing at the boulders in the distance. "Is this what you're looking for?"

The future king took the box and opened it. It was the flashlight. He lifted the hand-sized apparatus and found a note in the box:

A LIGHTNING FLASH BLINKS IN THE NIGHT
AND ALL THE EARTH IS MOMENTARILY IN SIGHT
AND WE WALK ON INTO THE DARK OF THE NIGHT
UNTIL ANOTHER FLASH SETS OUR PATH ALIGHT

*

VESSELS
OF LIGHT

• • • • • • • • • • •

Acknowledgments

A NUDGE HERE and a thwack there, a shove now and a tug then, a whisper, a bellow—in varied forms—events, things, and especially people—had set my feet to take the first big step, my hands to type the first word. They were each a vessel of light—often voyaging on a separate line of causality from mine—that ferried this book to where it is now. Endless thanks:

Fred, you brought my language into this world some thirty years ago. Eugene, you "warned" that I must give you the first autographed book when I write (this was over ten years ago when I had not an inkling of ever writing a novel). Dan and Mich—the first to read my experimentations—your input helped to shape my writing from the outset. Jason, Paul, and Uei Lim, you did not kill me for leaving my lucrative career as a creative director to embark on this. Corinne, my big sis, you've always whispered practical wisdom to me through the years. Lisa, you said, "I admire your courage" at the time when a part of me was calling myself "foolish" (not that I'm not). Jamie, Mike, Paul, Ely, and Min, your voluntary part in the little focus group helped to shape the marketing vision of this book. Bro John, you've been a beacon of light, a mentor, and a brother. LB, my big brother, you described my work as "a good Burgundy terroir"—that was deeply affirming coming from you.

CZ—agent, co-pilot, reader, and listener—you believed in my work from day one. Nicole—editor of "Lemonade Revealed"—you edified me with your professionalism and persistency. (Proofreaders:) Mike, your sharing of time and talent is a flashlight in the dark. Reuben, you selflessly fielded an exhaustive email after reading the first manuscript. Diane and Joanne, your sleights of hand had taken "Lemonade Revealed" to finesse.

Sherry
—my wife—
your support,
spoken or otherwise,
silenced the many storms
that came my way.

PADDLE WITH ALL YOUR HEART…
[BUT] IT IS THE HORIZON
THAT COMES TO YOU.